THIEF of
HEARTS

OTHER BOOKS BY LAURENCE YEP

Sweetwater

Dragonwings
A 1976 Newbery Honor Book

Child of the Owl

The Serpent's Children

Mountain Light

The Rainbow People

Tongues of Jade

Dragon's Gate
A 1994 Newbery Honor Book

DRAGON OF THE LOST SEA FANTASIES

Dragon of the Lost Sea

Dragon Steel

Dragon Cauldron

Dragon War

EDITED BY LAURENCE YEP

American Dragons
Twenty-Five Asian American Voices

LAURENCE YEP

THIEF of HEARTS

HarperCollins*Publishers*

Library of Congress Cataloging-in-Publication Data
Yep, Laurence.
    Thief of hearts / Laurence Yep.
        p.   cm.
    Summary: When Stacy is paired with a Chinese girl at school who is accused of theft,
she must come to terms with her own Chinese and American heritage.
    ISBN 0-06-025341-X. — ISBN 0-06-025342-8 (lib. bdg.)
    1. Chinese Americans—Fiction.   2. Grandmothers—Fiction.   3. Family life—
Fiction.   4. Friendship—Fiction.   5. Stealing—Fiction.   6. Chinatown (San Francisco,
Calif.)—Fiction   I. Title.
PZ7.Y44Th   1995   94-18703
[Fic]—dc20   CIP
                                                                              AC

Typography by Christine Hoffman Casarsa
2   3   4   5   6   7   8   9   10
❖

for Joanne

One

"Whoa, you're not taking cold spareribs to school." Mom sprang to the refrigerator faster than a speeding bullet.

I held on to the Tupperware container of the delicious spareribs that Tai-Paw, my great-grandmother, had made. "They've got a microwave in the teachers' lounge, and for a rib Mrs. Anderson will let me heat them up."

"Right." Mom snatched the container out of my hands and put it back in the refrigerator. "And if you think I believe that one, try selling me the Golden Gate Bridge. You can take some salad. Your dad made it for you special."

"He makes it with raw vegetables, and they're too crunchy. Last time I almost broke a filling on a carrot." Putting my hand into the pocket of my jeans, I figured I had enough money for lunch, so I started to ease toward the door.

Mom must have eyes in the back of her head, though, because she reached behind her and caught me without even looking. "A slice of pizza and a Coke are *not* a good meal."

"Neither is ice cream," I pointed out. "But you've been known to binge."

Mom did what she always does when she is losing an argument: She changed the topic. Getting out another Tupperware container, she filled it with rabbit food, got a plastic fork, and put it all into a paper bag. "Get home early tonight, will you? We really ought to eat together more often. I talked to your dad, and we'll both make efforts to have meals as a family. In any case, I need you to put on the rice."

It was a small enough chore, but it was the principle of the thing. After all, I had to be free to handle important stuff. "Can't Tai-Paw do it?"

Mom's voice took on the sharp, disapproving edge that I'd heard so often. "Tai-Paw is *not* our maid," she snapped.

Mom was right. I did take Tai-Paw for granted. She was always this friendly but alien presence. Most of the time she stayed in her room watching the Chinese cable stations on TV. Feeling guilty, I promised. "Okay, the rice will be ready."

Mom fiddled with her charm bracelet the way

she did whenever she was ill at ease. The little jade owl danced as she played with it. "Honestly, sometimes I don't know what's wrong with you. You were the one who complained that we never did things together."

I was going to say that she was the psychologist, but I bit my tongue. After all, it would be nice to eat together for a change. We were all so busy that we rarely got to do things as a family. "Sorry," I said. I seemed to be apologizing to my mother almost every day for some failure.

"'Sorry' doesn't hack it," Mom said snippily. "Think before you speak, and only say something when you mean it."

I threw up my hands in unconditional surrender. "Even when I agree with you and apologize, I'm in the wrong."

As I headed for my bicycle in the garage, Mom stopped me. "I'm sorry, honey. This isn't the way I meant to start out your day."

I merely grunted. "I know, you have a lot on your mind."

She fussed over my collar like she used to do when I was small. Then I had liked the attention; but as I grew older, I came to see it as yet another form of criticism. "You've got high school next year," Mom said, "and college will be coming up before you know it. You have to learn to apply yourself more. We won't always be around to bail you out."

I pulled away. "I can handle things. I just may not do it your way."

Mom turned her fussiness to her bracelet instead, jiggling the little owl charm. "You're not as grown-up as you think."

I tried to remember the last time Mom and I'd had a pleasant, comfortable chat, and couldn't. "The rice will be ready," I said, and threw her a salute.

Mom turned me toward the front door. "You don't need to ride your bike today. Your dad will take you to school, and you can catch a bus home with Hong Ch'un."

Dad never gave me a lift to school. My parents were obviously up to something. "Who's Hong Ch'un?"

Mom rushed over to the counter to cram some exam papers into her briefcase. "You remember Mr. Wang? The one who works with your dad?"

I recalled a Chinese man in his late thirties with very good posture and a nervous laugh. "Yeah. The Chinese guy who couldn't talk to anyone in Chinese."

Hastily Mom began hunting through a pile of papers on the table. "Now I know those lecture notes are here somewhere." As she searched, she went on.

"Mr. Wang speaks Mandarin, the Chinese dialect from up north. We speak Cantonese." Or rather, Mom and her friends did. "Well, he's brought his wife and daughter over from China. We thought it would be nice to have dinner with the Wangs tonight."

So I was going to get caught in another one of Mom's Chinese love fests. As Dad said, you can take the girl out of Chinatown, but you can't take the Chinatown out of the girl. Even though we now lived some fifty miles south of San Francisco's Chinatown, Mom still tried to recapture the feeling of her old neighborhood. If anyone from Chinatown moved into Almaden, she made a point of snaring them and including them in her network of ex-Chinatowners, and lately she had been broadening her invitations to include anyone Chinese, no matter where they came from.

Mom and Dad weren't trying to have dinner with me after all. "Thanks," I said resentfully. "Thanks a lot."

"Now don't pout," Mom chided me. "Hong Ch'un is thirteen, so she should be in your class at middle school. I know you'll make her feel welcome." It was a warning.

I sulked by the counter. "Does she even speak English?"

In triumph, she slid a folder of papers from the pile and shoved it into her briefcase. "Mr. Wang says she does." Mom snatched up her car keys, but before she could start toward her car, Tai-Paw called to her. "You forgot your sweater."

Since Tai-Paw was ninety, her hair was almost all white, and I knew from photos that she had once been plump. However, she was now thin, having lost weight during her long recovery from a broken hip. Liver spots dotted her cheeks and hands like large freckles. Even so, her eyes were as lively as ever.

Though the morning was mild, she was armored against the cold. A long-sleeved knit sweater covered her arms up to her wrists and was buttoned up to her neck.

Tai-Paw shuffled forward in her slippers, holding out a white fluffy sweater. Though her broken hip had mended, she had never regained her full mobility. "Here you are."

"Thank you," Mom said meekly, putting down her things before she took the sweater. She might manage a whole psych department at the junior college, give papers around the world, and act as consultant to a lot of big companies, but she would always be a little girl to her grandmother.

I went over to kiss Tai-Paw on the cheek. I liked

her, though I didn't always understand her—and I think the reverse was also true. "What are you doing up so early, Tai-Paw?"

She patted me on the shoulder. "I never sleep for long now, so I thought I'd come out and say hello to your visitors."

"You're going to do that?" I asked, surprised. When my friends came to visit, she was usually so subdued.

"There'll be plenty of time for that this afternoon," Mom said as she pulled the sweater over her head.

Tai-Paw fussed over her, tugging Mom's hair from underneath the sweater out through the collar. "Their situation reminds me of someone. They might be lonely."

When you really came down to it, I didn't know much about Tai-Paw or how she felt about stuff. I had never even stopped to consider that she might be lonely. "Does Hong Ch'un remind you of yourself when you first came here?"

"No," Tai-Paw said, straightening Mom's sweater and sleeves as if she were a large doll. "Of your mother. When she first came to live with me in Chinatown. She wasn't born there, you know."

"So she had to adjust." That was news to me about my mom. I guess I didn't think much about her, either.

"And Chinatown had to adjust to her." She glanced at Mom. "And to your husband. Remember the time you went into that restaurant in Chinatown?"

"That's in the past." Mom shrugged. She obviously wanted to forget.

Since Mom was no help, I prompted Tai-Paw. "What happened?"

Tai-Paw squatted slowly and picked up Mom's briefcase. "Your mother and father went into this place to eat. But the waiter wouldn't wait on them. The manager had to send someone else over."

"Why?" It was hard to see what my parents could have done that would have offended him. I mean, they were, well, boring.

Mom hurriedly took the briefcase from Tai-Paw. "We were what is politely called a mixed couple."

"When I heard about it, I set that waiter and that manager straight," Tai-Paw declared. "Next week we had a big banquet for free."

"I would have liked to have seen that." I grinned. I could just picture her storming into the restaurant.

Mom scratched her neck as if she were already getting too hot. "I'd still like to know how you found out. We never said a word to you."

Tai-Paw tapped the back of Mom's hand to make her stop scratching. "Well, it won't do any harm now. Mr. Jeh was a dishwasher at the restaurant. When he heard the commotion, he peeked through the kitchen doors and saw you."

"Mr. Jeh?" Mom asked, astounded. She began trying to calculate figures in her head. "But he must have been . . ."

Tai-Paw inspected Mom one last time. "Very old. He just retired this year. And only because the new owners were idiots."

"Well, thank you," Mom said, and gave her a quick hug. "But you don't have to fight my battles for me anymore."

Tai-Paw hugged her back. "You work too hard. I'll talk to your boss again."

Mom let her go. "I don't think Dean Standish has recovered from your last conversation with him."

"He shouldn't have made me mad," Tai-Paw declared. I could never get either her or my parents to tell the complete story of the day when Mom had made the mistake of showing her workplace to Tai-Paw.

"Next time pick something cheaper to break," Mom said, and cocked her head when she heard the car horn. "That'll be your father. Come on."

"Wait. Help me put on my bandanna," Tai-Paw said. From her pants pocket, she pulled a colorful silken scarf.

"Is your rheumatism acting up?" Mom asked sympathetically.

"We must be in for rain," Tai-Paw sighed.

Tucking her briefcase under her arm, Mom tied the bandanna under Tai-Paw's chin. She was determined to stay as pale as the day several years ago when Mom had rescued her from Uncle Phil's clutches. She had been living with Uncle Phil up in San Francisco, but neither he nor she had been very happy with the arrangement. So even though we were miles from Chinatown, Tai-Paw had been glad to come down here. However, she said a tan would make her look like a field hand to her friends.

As we went outside, Tai-Paw shook off our attempts to aid her. "What do you think I am? Old?"

Mom smiled. "I was going to lean on you for support." She kept pace beside her, ready to catch Tai-Paw if she faltered.

Dad was in a clean white shirt and tie, but as usual he had forgotten to comb his blond hair, so it stuck up in little tufts while he sat at the wheel of his car. If Mom was a lightning bolt, all tense and crackling with energy, Dad was a big, boisterous teddy bear.

When he saw Tai-Paw, he got out of the car immediately. In some ways, he got on with Tai-Paw even better than Mom did. "Tai-Paw, what are you doing out here?"

"Hello, hello," Tai-Paw called, and waved to the people in the car. In the backseat was Mr. Wang with a

Chinese woman in her late thirties. I hadn't expected the entire family. Next to them was a girl about my age, but her hair had been twisted into a braid on either side of her head, and she wore a plain white blouse and dark black skirt.

"This is Mrs. Low. Officially, I'm her grandson-in-law, but I think of myself as her adopted grandson," Dad said to the Wangs.

When the Wangs nodded their heads, I saw that the girl's hair was done up with Snoopy barrettes. As I started to snicker, Mom shot me a warning look, so I quickly made my face blank.

Dad finished the introductions. "You already met Mr. Wang, but this is his wife. And this is their daughter, Hong Ch'un."

While Mom hovered attentively at her side, Tai-Paw spread her arms. "Welcome."

"It's nice to see you." Mr. Wang smiled. He spoke with difficulty though, as if there were marbles in his mouth while he tried to form the English syllables.

Dad indicated Mom. "And you remember my wife, Casey, and our daughter, Stacy." Mom waved hello as she got into her car.

Mrs. Wang had sat in dignified silence up until then—like a spectator at a play where the actors are bumbling across the stage. However, Hong Ch'un's eyes swung toward me and, though she kept her face blank, I could see the surprise in her eyes. Most of my parents' Chinese visitors have the same reaction the first time they catch sight of me.

Though I have Dad's blond hair and pale skin, I have Mom's Chinese eyes—the old epicanthic fold, he calls it. There's a muscle or something that pulls up the corners of my eyes like it does for Asians.

As Mom pulled away, Hong Ch'un stared at me as if I were an exhibit in a sideshow. Her eyes flicked from my hair to my eyes as she said something in Chinese.

I smiled politely, the way I always did when one of Mom's Chinese friends tried to speak Chinese to me— though Hong Ch'un's sounded a little flatter than theirs. "Sorry. I only speak English and Spanish."

"And you wouldn't understand anyway," Mr. Wang said quickly. "We only speak Mandarin, and your mother only Cantonese." Cantonese was the dialect spoken in the south of China, while Mandarin was spoken in the north.

Hong Ch'un looked at me in horror as if I had just confessed to murdering someone with an ax. "Why don't you speak Cantonese at least?"

I pressed my lips into a thin smile, reminding myself to be patient. Mom's Chinese friends had asked similar questions, but it never got any easier to answer them. "I don't have much chance to practice it here."

"I learned English in China," Hong Ch'un argued.

"Chinese is . . . is beautiful and noble." She paused as she struggled to put her words into English. I had the same trouble when I tried to speak Chinese. "It's what makes you Chinese."

Our school has a pretty active exchange program with other countries, so I'd met exchange students from Europe and Africa and Latin America, and I'd gotten along with them all by trying to see things from their viewpoints. So I attempted to see hers now. And I guess if I had been born in China, I would have felt that way, but I had been born here. "I'm not Chinese," I tried to explain. "I'm an American."

Her mouth worked in frustration. Trying to hold a discussion was like trying to run in glue. "But you lose so much."

"It's what we've told her," Dad said over his shoulder. "There's a group that has a little Chinese school every Saturday."

Mr. Wang, however, leaped to my defense. "No, Stacy is right. In America, you have to be an American."

"I don't see why you can't be both," Dad suggested.

It was a compromise that satisfied no one.

Hong Ch'un stared at me in disgust. "You should go to that school."

I tried to remind myself that she was fresh from another culture, so I just tried to put her off. "Sometime."

However, there wasn't much "give" to Hong Ch'un.

She sighed and shook her head. "Not sometime. To-morrow."

It's funny how two people can rub one another the wrong way. I know the American way isn't the only one, so I was willing to listen and learn. But none of the exchange students I had met had had Hong Ch'un's superior attitude. "Don't tell me what to do, all right?"

Several times Hong Ch'un attempted to say something, but her English just wasn't up to the complexity of her thoughts. So instead, she emphasized her points by sometimes exaggerating what she did say. "Everyone here is so-o-o spoiled."

I didn't see where she got off calling Americans names. "What makes you so high and mighty?" I demanded.

"You waste everything here," she said with a contemptuous shake of her head.

I was about to tell her she was welcome to go back to China when Mr. Wang spoke to her sharply in Chinese—so she satisfied herself with another shake of her head and said nothing more. And that ended our argument in slow motion.

"Hong Ch'un is very excited about school," Mr. Wang said to break the silence.

When I didn't say anything either, Dad spoke up. "I can imagine."

"Hong Ch'un was a very good student back home." Mr. Wang glanced at his daughter, and when she didn't answer, he plowed on resolutely. "She hopes her English is adequate here."

Dad waited for me to say something and then responded for me. "From what I heard on the way here, her English seems very good."

"My daughter hopes to make a good impression," Mr. Wang said, speaking for Hong Ch'un.

"Stacy was nervous on her first day," Dad said, and prompted me, "Weren't you, Stacy?" When I didn't answer, he just charged on.

For the next few minutes, Hong Ch'un and I carried on a conversation by proxy—and, according to our fathers, having a grand old time already.

"Did you leave any family in China?" Tai-Paw asked.

"Some," Mr. Wang said carefully.

"My grandmother," Hong Ch'un added with a resentful glance at her father. "She spoke English with hardly a trace of an accent."

"She wouldn't come," Mr. Wang hurriedly supplied.

"Ah," Tai-Paw sighed sadly.

I thought I'd better get the show on the road, so I kissed Tai-Paw on the cheek. "'Bye, Tai-Paw. See you later."

"Yes, thank you," Tai-Paw said absently, as if she were thinking of that other old lady stuck back in China. "Have a good day in school," she wished as she turned to shuffle back inside.

With my backpack in my hands, I went around to the passenger side of the front seat and got in. I'd no sooner set my bag on my lap when the door of the house next to us flew open, and Karen plunged outside. Karen was a short, plump blonde with a taste for rugby shirts.

Karen had been my friend since first grade, always letting me decide on the games and telling her what to do. One time Dad called her my shadow. I felt guilty in some ways that I didn't have more time for her nowadays.

"Wait, Dad," I said.

Dad, though, started to back up. "Sorry, hon. There's no more room."

Through the window, I mouthed an apology to Karen, and she stopped, jacket in one hand, book bag in the other, looking forlorn.

Two

Dad swung the car out into the street and around the corner, accelerating as he went past the tract homes. Tai-Paw once told me that they reminded her of cakes scattered on green lawns.

Hong Ch'un had turned to watch the ranch houses slide by. On her face, I saw a faraway look that I recognized from the time when I'd been a counselor at the summer Y camp. She was homesick, I realized. "Do you miss home very much?"

She eyed me coldly—as if my pity were almost an insult to her. "At home, we lived in part of a prince's palace. We had a real orchard, and our garden was ten times as big as this."

I couldn't begin to understand what it was like to step down from that scale of grandeur to the little backyards we had here in Almaden. "Everything must seem very strange here," I tried to sympathize.

"Very strange," she agreed wholeheartedly.

Mr. Wang spoke furiously to his daughter until her cheeks were a bright red, and she didn't say another word during the rest of the trip. That was fine by me; and I think we were both grateful when Dad pulled up to Mercury Middle School.

"Did you know that the Chinese worked the mercury mines here in Almaden?" Dad asked. "That's why the teams are called the Miners."

"No. Isn't that interesting, Hong Ch'un?" Mr. Wang asked, and got no more reply than he had before.

The middle school spread out over a couple of acres with long, low rectangular buildings painted colors bright enough for building blocks. A river of bicycles poured onto the campus while a stream of cars flowed into its parking lot. Some kids took the shortcut, tearing across the lawn, and were shouted at by the gardeners. There were the bookies—the drudges who stayed stuck in their books—and there were the mods, who wore the latest clothes.

The Wangs' eyes grew large as they watched the spectacle, but they said nothing. Once Dad had stopped, I left the car, eager to make my escape, but even then I couldn't be free. "Show her where the office is, hon," Dad said.

I waited as her parents spoke to her in Mandarin. With a curt nod, Hong Ch'un slammed the door shut.

"Hey, Stace!" Jeff rattled by on his skateboard in his T-shirt and long shorts decorated with pink bowling pins. With his backpack swinging on his back and long blond hair flying, he barely missed Sylvia, who, with her bobbed hair dyed black and her cadaverous makeup, looked almost like a vampire.

"Watch it, you maniac!" she snapped.

Jeff jumped off his skateboard, catching the rear with his foot so that the skateboard flipped into the air, where he neatly caught it. "Who pickled you today? I've got just the thing to cheer you up." He reached into his backpack with a confident grin and lifted something out in his fist. "Look at what Cindy gave me. We're going to call it Barrows." Mr. Barrows was the vice-principal.

He set it down on the pavement and lifted his hand away, revealing a little pink kangaroo. "Doesn't it look like him?"

Sylvia leaned forward to study it. "Yeah, I think it's the nose."

Jeff wound it up and then released it. Immediately the kangaroo crashed its cymbals together as it hopped about and wiggled its tail. "Barrows dances like that too." As Sylvia started to laugh, Jeff grinned. "Just call me Dr. Sunshine, bringing rays of joy to boys and girls everywhere."

Sylvia smiled when she saw me. "Oh, Stacy, thank

heaven. Please, please, please say you did the math last night," she begged.

"I notice you don't ask me," Jeff said, retrieving his toy.

"Right, like only if I want to flunk." Sylvia shrugged.

"Number three was a killer," I warned as I took off my backpack and took my homework from my binder.

"You're a lifesaver." Sylvia knelt, balancing my homework on one knee.

Behind me, I heard my father give a gentle toot as a reminder. "This is Hong Ch'un," I said, indicating her.

"Nice to meetcha," Sylvia said without looking up.

"See you tonight," Dad called.

"Right, Dad." I crouched slightly, waving a good-bye to him. He finally got the hint and started up his engine again.

"Good luck. Have fun today," Dad yelled. Mr. Wang was still waving good-bye as they swung around the curve toward the exit.

As Sylvia hastily began to write down the answers, she asked, "So, Stace, see the flick last night? Fab."

"What station?" I asked, waving hello to a couple of other friends.

"I dunno." Sylvia shrugged. "One of the cables, I think. It was all about these Siamese twins parted at

20

birth. Real spooky. One was normal and the other was real creep-o. And the sick one wants to be the only one and tries to kill the good one."

"So who was in it?" I asked.

Sylvia scratched her head. She was never too good on details. "Let's see. Somebody you like. Cute guy."

I gave an exasperated click of my tongue. "How can you ace English and be so lousy on the important things?"

"I can't help it," Sylvia said.

"I still wouldn't mind going over the history notes with you," I said. We had a killer exam coming up on Friday.

Sylvia's voice rose a tone higher as she said play-fully, "Sure, but there's only one way to ace it."

Sylvia swore by her lucky charm. "You don't think a rabbit's foot is really going to help you?" I asked.

"It's always come through up to now." Sylvia gave it a loud kiss. "Haven't you, baby?" She held it out to me.

I touched it with a fingertip. "You've probably spread more flu germs by having people kiss your rabbit's foot."

"Come Friday morning, you'll be *begging* to kiss my rabbit's foot too." When she handed me back the homework, she sprang to her feet. "Tootles."

"See you in class," I called after her. I figured that

I'd dump Hong Ch'un in the office and be done with her.

Mr. Barrows, the vice-principal, was a balding, middle-aged man with wire-rim glasses. He always gave the impression of being an incomplete picture because there was always something untidy about him— either his shirttail was hanging loose or his shoelaces were untied.

"Well, your records are most impressive," he said to Hong Ch'un, consulting a file. "We have some evaluative tests for you to take, but in the meantime you can go to class with Stacy so you can get acclimated."

That was the last thing I needed. "Some of my classes are advanced ones. They may be pretty hard for a newcomer, sir."

"I can keep up," Hong Ch'un insisted.

Mr. Barrows smiled at me. "I know Stacy will make you feel comfortable. Did you bring a combination lock, Hong Ch'un?"

When Hong Ch'un shook her head, Mr. Barrows closed the file. "Do you know what one is?"

Hong Ch'un stiffened. "Of course."

He smiled apologetically. "You can get one at any hardware store. In the meantime, maybe Stacy will share her locker with you."

Hong Ch'un stood where she was. She was as keen about the notion as I was. "It isn't necessary."

"Nonsense." Mr. Barrows smiled. "You don't mind, do you, Stacy?"

"It isn't necessary," Hong Ch'un repeated.

With a shrug, Mr. Barrows shoved a sheet of paper toward her. "Well, here's your list of room assignments. Just follow Stacy."

"It isn't necessary."

Mr. Barrows glanced at her and then at me. "Is there some problem I don't know about?"

"I don't need help," Hong Ch'un said, and glared at me. Actually she meant she didn't want *my* help.

"What have I done to you?" I asked.

"My father ordered me to be nice to you," she said.

"Thank you for being very gracious," I said sarcastically.

Hong Ch'un, though, didn't realize I was joking. "Your father is a very good friend to mine." From her frown, she didn't relish the role.

"Don't do me any favors," I snapped.

She stiffened as if insulted. "You don't want my friendship? All Chinese are supposed to stick together."

"I don't call it friendship to badger me like you did in the car," I said.

"I know Hong Ch'un didn't mean anything," Mr. Barrows said quickly.

I shook my head. "We just don't get along, Mr.

Barrows. I think you ought to get someone else to help her today."

"But you're the best person for the job," he insisted.

I pressed my hand against the skin below my throat. "Why?"

If Mr. Barrows had explained that I was good with newcomers, he might have won me over. Instead, he pressed his fingertips together and said, "Well, she is Chinese."

"So?" I asked. "I just met her this morning. I don't know her."

"You're both Chinese." Mr. Barrows could be as pigheaded as my mother. "That is, your mother is Chinese," he said. He knew her well from PTA meetings.

"Southern Chinese," I corrected him. "And Hong Ch'un is northern. We've got as much in common as you would with an African."

"I have been to Nigeria three times." Mr. Barrows indicated several photos on the wall. "I am proud to claim an African heritage. I'm surprised at you, Stacy."

All my life I thought I was just like everyone else. In fact, that's the way I still feel. So it was a shock to find out that people didn't share the same opinion.

"It's not fair to lump me in with her, sir," I said stubbornly. "You should pick me out for my abilities, not for the way I look. Would you want someone to ask you to do something on that basis?"

"I've picked you because you are the best possible choice for the job," he said firmly.

I felt cornered and that, in turn, made me feel frustrated. "Why?" Tactically, it was a bad mistake.

"My grandmother was a teacher. My parents were both teachers. I tried to be a car salesman." From his suit pocket he pulled an old-fashioned fountain pen— the kind you had to fill up with ink. "I bet you think I carry this around because I'm too cheap to buy a new pen."

I rolled my eyes, because he found a way to tell this story to every student who wound up in his clutches.

Mr. Barrows fingered the pen affectionately. "This was my grandfather's. His first class gave it to him." The pride in his eyes was obvious as he set it down again. "I could no more avoid my vocation than my heritage."

I knew that the only way to avoid a longer lecture was to agree with him. "Yes, sir."

Outside his office, Hong Ch'un whirled. "I don't like being paired with a *t'ung chung*, either."

It was a term I had never heard Mom or Tai-Paw use. However, from her tone, I knew it was meant to be an insult. "A what?"

"So you're deaf, too." And she used the name again

before she stalked away, much to my relief.

At that moment I felt a tap on my shoulder. "I thought we were supposed to ride to school together."

I turned to see Karen. "It was my parents' idea to go to school with that new girl, Hong Ch'un. They sprang it on me at the last moment so I couldn't tell you. Sorry."

"It's okay." She shrugged. "Would you like to do some homework together?" She continued in a small voice, "Like in the old days?" I was going to tell her no, but she added, "You haven't come to visit me in a long time."

"I do all the time," I said.

She shook her head. "You used to."

I tried to remember the last time I had visited Karen at night—any night—and realized that I couldn't. It wasn't intentional. I'd simply gotten involved in all different kinds of activities. Maybe I took her for granted as much I did Tai-Paw.

All right, she was a little odd—but not very much if you considered her parents. And she was so sweet and helpful that I didn't want to hurt her feelings any more than I already had. "How about tomorrow?" I suggested.

"What about tonight?" she asked.

"I have to appease the parental units and baby-sit

Hong Ch'un and her family." I sighed.

"It's okay," Karen said, but she looked disappointed.

But it wasn't okay with me. "I'll make it up to you sometime," I promised.

"Sure," Karen said doubtfully.

However, in our first class, the teacher, Mr. Arnold, made Karen move her seat.

I glanced at Karen. We hadn't made any trouble. (All right, so maybe we did talk a little and giggle a little; but is that a crime?)

"I want you to help our new classmate adjust," said Mr. Arnold. He turned to address the class. "Hong Ch'un has just arrived from China. Mr. Barrows said from Beijing, in fact." When he glanced at her, she nodded confirmation. Motioning for her to take a seat, Mr. Arnold headed toward the front of the classroom. "Stacy, will you share your textbook with Hong Ch'un?"

From the look of distaste on her face, Hong Ch'un didn't like the idea any more than I did.

Karen already had her things in her arms and got up. "Have fun," she muttered.

"I won't," I said as I slumped in my chair. Suddenly I felt like I was in Sylvia's movie; I could understand the impulse to kill an unwanted twin.

Three

In the next class that morning, Ms. Armstrong also made sure I sat next to Hong Ch'un so I could share my books with her and help her adjust. It made me feel as if I were under a curse for the rest of the morning.

On the way to our next class, Jeff clapped a hand on my shoulder. "Why so glum, chum?"

"The teachers keep sticking me with the pickle of all pickles," I said.

"She's not very nice," Karen said from behind us.

Jeff ignored Karen, the way most kids did at Merc. In fact, most of them didn't know who she was if I mentioned her name. It was as if she were the Invisible Girl.

I made a point of smiling at her. "You got that right."

Jeff barely glanced at her as he reached into his backpack with a confident grin. "Dr. Sunshine to the rescue." But after a moment the grin became a grimace as he began to rummage around frantically in his bag. Finally he opened the flap and began taking out books, notepads, and other interesting junk, including one old knitting needle. "My toy's gone."

Sylvia combed her hair from her face with her hands. "Cheer up. It's bound to turn up."

Jeff glumly shook his now-empty backpack over the concrete path.

He flung the bag down in disgust. "It reminded me of a toy I had when I was a kid." He slapped his forehead. "I told Cindy that, when I saw it in the store window, and she got it for me. She's gonna kill me."

"Maybe you can buy another to replace it," I suggested sympathetically.

He tapped his pockets. "No dinero."

Beneath all of Jeff's wackiness was a genuine desire to make people happy. I realized with a start that Jeff had been my friend almost as long as Karen. I took him for granted too. "I'll loan you the money."

"You will?" he asked in surprise.

I started to reach for my wallet. "How much?"

He thought about it for a moment and then began to stuff his things back into his pack. "Naw, I couldn't. It doesn't seem right to borrow money from one girl to replace a present bought by another girl."

"And Cindy would hound you beyond the grave if she found out," Sylvia added.

Jeff anxiously sprang to his feet. "You're not going to tell, are you?"

"What's it worth to you?" Sylvia asked as we began walking again to our next class.

"I told you I don't have any money," Jeff protested.

"Fine, you can pay me back in services." Sylvia began to tick off the items on her fingers. "You can mow our lawn and . . ."

As she listed the items, Jeff groaned. "This is extortion."

"No, extortion is where I threaten to break your legs if you don't mow my lawn." Sylvia batted her eyelashes in mock flirtation. "The proper term for what I'm doing to you is *blackmail*."

However, it was Sylvia's turn to panic in government class when Ms. Sims announced a surprise quiz.

I had been paired yet again with Hong Ch'un, so I didn't notice Sylvia at first. Suddenly there was a cascade of clunks behind me. I turned to see that Sylvia had overturned her bag. Books, pens, and lipstick spilled off the desktop onto the floor. "I can't find my rabbit's foot."

"You had it this morning," I said.

Sylvia squatted down, fingers splayed outward as

she swept her hands over the linoleum. "It's got to be here somewhere. Help me look."

Ms. Sims was coming over. "You can buy another after school," I said.

Sylvia straightened up with a wail. "But the test is now."

Jeff touched Sylvia's shoulder. "Come on. Get back in your seat."

Sylvia shot up and grabbed his vest. "If you stole it, Jeff . . ."

Jeff shoved her away. "I'm not that desperate."

Ms. Sims loomed over Sylvia. "Put that trash away and get ready for the test."

I slipped out of my desk and knelt beside Sylvia, who shot a grateful look at me. "Can you believe that Jeff? I bet he's trying to weasel out of our deal."

"It'll turn up," I tried to reassure her. She'd probably find her lucky charm in another pocket, and the windup kangaroo had probably fallen out of Jeff's backpack.

Sylvia slapped the linoleum miserably. "You can't trust anyone these days."

After we had passed the completed quizzes forward, I looked behind me toward Sylvia. Mutely she shook her head and then, resting her elbows on the desktop, buried her face against her arms.

People lose little things every day, and at first I assigned the losses to coincidence. But then Mr. Barrows came on the public address system.

"Fun is fun," declared Mr. Barrows, sounding too annoyed to enjoy what might be a joke. "But will the person or persons who stole my pen return it to me? It has little monetary value, but it is worth an immense amount in sentiment. Whoever has stolen it has taken a little bit of my heart. If the pen is left in my box, I will not ask any questions."

Everyone started to chuckle because at some time we all had heard the story about the pen. Mr. Barrows used it to make a point on everything but the law of gravity.

However, everyone sobered up when Mr. Barrows added, "If this polite request is not honored, I will have to take more forceful measures."

Instantly people turned around to stare at Jeff, because he was always playing pranks. Helplessly he placed his hands upon his chest. "I didn't take it. For once, I'm innocent."

Sylvia looked up from her desk. "Maybe I didn't lose my rabbit's foot. Maybe somebody took it."

"And my windup toy," Jeff said.

"Unless," Sylvia said darkly, "you staged the theft to throw off suspicion."

"Jeff's jokes are never mean," I said to her. "But these thefts are just plain malicious."

Jeff nodded. "They may seem like nothing, but the things that were stolen were important to the owners."

"Who knew about the toy?" Sylvia demanded.

"I was playing with it most of the morning." Jeff shrugged. "So it'd be just about everybody."

Sylvia sighed. "Everyone knows about my rabbit's foot."

"You too?" another girl asked. "I lost one of my piano earrings." She indicated a cheap plastic hoop. "They were a souvenir of my visit to the Liberace Museum."

Mr. Barrows's announcement made other people compare their losses. They were all silly things—a ribbon, a sticker on a binder. It was nothing you could go to the police about. The monetary value was probably less than five bucks; but you couldn't put a price tag on the sentimental value.

If Jeff hadn't lost his toy, I would have said he was the likely culprit, but he had been just as upset as Sylvia. I sympathized with him, of course, just as I did with Sylvia and my other friends who had lost their treasures. At the start of lunch period, I even said something to Mr. Barrows about his loss.

"I can't understand," he complained to me. "It's not

33

worth anything." He held out a hand to me. "Stacy, everyone in the school listens to you. Spread the word. If this is a joke, it isn't funny. I just want my pen back."

I felt sorry for Mr. Barrows. "I will," I promised, but it would have to be tomorrow. Today I was more nervous about having to entertain Hong Ch'un. As a result, though the whole campus was buzzing about the thefts, I decided to try to patch up things with Hong Ch'un over lunch.

When the bell rang, Karen asked me her usual question: "So where do you want to have lunch?"

I made a point of including Hong Ch'un. "Where would you like to eat, Hong Ch'un?" I asked her.

Hong Ch'un seemed surprised by the invitation. Almost shyly she said, "Somewhere where it's green."

"We could sit under the oak tree," I suggested. "That way we could have shade."

On the lawn in front of the school was an old tree even older than Merc itself. It had huge roots, and its branches were as thick as my waist.

From her lunch bag, Hong Ch'un pulled one of those crullerlike Chinese doughnuts that are really salty. And in her other hand she had a fat, squat little plastic thermos of what I thought was tea until she dipped the doughnut into it and took a bite.

When I glanced into the thermos I saw that it held homemade rice porridge. "Having *jook*?" I asked conversationally.

"We call rice porridge *chu*," she corrected me.

"Well, we call it *jook*," I explained. I thought my mother's dialect was just as good as hers. "Did they have many trees where you lived?"

"I lived in the heart of the city." She swirled the doughnut around in the porridge. "If I wanted trees, I went to the park. I like climbing."

"There used to be trees all around here, but now they're mostly gone. But when I was a kid, I was a regular squirrel." I grinned weakly at her. She said nothing, but she had a thoughtful look, as if she were searching for something else to say and keep the conversation going. So I knew that I had made contact somehow.

She sampled my lunch, but she shared my opinion that Dad had made rabbit's food. Throughout lunch, Karen kept eating steadily. Hong Ch'un's eyes widened when she saw Karen begin to eat a second fat sandwich. "You shouldn't eat so much," Hong Ch'un scolded. "It isn't good for you."

Karen deliberately crammed half of the sandwich into her mouth. "You need lessons in being polite."

I tried to smooth things over. "She comes from a

different culture with different customs."

Karen looked at me with those hurt, puppy-dog eyes of hers. "She's in America now, so she ought to learn some American manners—just like she shouldn't wear kiddy barrettes in her hair."

Hong Ch'un's hand shot up to one of her Snoopy barrettes. "What's wrong with these?"

Karen was normally very sweet unless you hurt her feelings. "They're only for five-year-olds."

"That's rude, Karen," I said. "You can't make fun of her just because she doesn't know our fashions." I sounded just like my mother.

With an angry look at me, Karen got up. "Well, she started it."

"Don't go away mad," I coaxed.

"I don't like the company you keep," she said over her shoulder, and walked away.

Hong Ch'un closed a hand around one of her pig-tails. "I wish you had told me."

"Sorry. I meant to tell you later," I said, crunching through another mouthful of lettuce. "I've got some rubber bands you could use."

Hong Ch'un hesitated and then dropped her hand. "No, I'll wear these for today," she said with dignity.

I capped my Tupperware. "Tell you what. Let's go to a rest room and I'll help you do your hair."

Hong Ch'un held on to one braid. "I suppose over here the barrettes are probably very cheap. But they were a gift from my grandmother. She heard that was what American girls wore over here. She obtained them with great difficulty because we were still in China."

"How did your grandmother get the barrettes?" I asked kindly.

"I don't know," Hong Ch'un said. "But things come in from Hong Kong and find their way to Beijing."

I felt bad for Hong Ch'un, and a little ashamed that I had felt superior to her about her wearing them. "I'm sorry."

"You're lucky to have your Tai-Paw," Hong Ch'un said wistfully and added, "I'm sorry too. Things are so different here. I don't mean to say the wrong things."

She wasn't so bad when she bent a little. "You'll learn," I said.

She looked away. "Sometimes I feel so lost. Father says I must change, but if I do, I think I will get even more lost."

"I guess it would be scary," I agreed.

Her head dipped slightly. "And this morning I met you: You don't want to have anything to do with what I value most. And if someone like you thinks that way, how will the others think?"

And I thought that *she* had been the one acting

superior. Maybe it was both of us. I had a lot to think about as we headed back to the lockers. There was a crowd around the lockers, including Karen, but when I tried to say hello to her, she merely glared. She still didn't forgive me.

With a sigh, I squatted down before my locker and opened it. "May I?" Hong Ch'un asked, and when I got out of the way, she took out her small backpack. As she lifted it up, something fell with a clink on the linoleum.

"You dropped something." Karen swiftly stooped and retrieved the object.

"Wait." I took it from Karen's hand. "Where did you get this?" I demanded from Hong Ch'un.

Hong Ch'un looked down at her backpack, bewildered. "I don't know."

I held up the object so everyone could see it. It was Mr. Barrows's pen. "I did not take it," she declared. "I did not take it."

Sylvia, who had the locker next to ours, snatched the backpack from Hong Ch'un. "That's mine!" Hong Ch'un cried.

Before Hong Ch'un could stop her, Sylvia had thrust a hand inside and pulled out a windup kangaroo. "Anybody recognize this?"

Jeff pushed his way through the gathering crowd. "Hey, that's my toy!"

Sylvia produced a rabbit's foot from the backpack. "So what's my lucky charm doing here?"

The crowd closed in at that point as others began going through the backpack. Hong Ch'un backed away until she bumped into the lockers.

I went over to her urgently. "How did that stuff get into your backpack?"

Hong Ch'un huddled into herself, shoulders raised, elbows tight against her sides. "I do not know. Someone must have put them there."

"Are you accusing me?" I asked.

She stiffened indignantly. "You are not saying *I* did it?"

"Who else?" demanded Sylvia. "It was your backpack."

"No, no! Please! You have to believe me!" She looked at the others. "I am no thief!" She got so excited that her thoughts got ahead of her tongue, and she began to speak in Chinese rather than in English.

Karen planted a fist on her hip. "Stacy, what kind of person is your new friend?"

"I am no thief," Hong Ch'un insisted, backing down the hallway. We watched her dart away until she turned the corner.

"There has to be an explanation for this," I said. "Hong Ch'un might lack tact, but she's no thief."

"Why did she run if she was innocent?" Sylvia was rubbing some dirt from her rabbit's foot.

"After all, the loot was in her bag," Jeff pointed out. "What more proof do you need?"

"I still think we ought to get her side of it," I argued. "In civics, they say you're supposed to be innocent until proven guilty."

Exasperated, Sylvia spread her arms. "You should be the last one to defend her. Because if it isn't her, then it has to be you. The stuff was in your locker."

"I don't need your lucky charm," I said.

"Well," Sylvia admitted, "I guess I can see why you'd side with her."

"What do you mean by that?" I demanded indignantly.

Sylvia jabbed her rabbit's foot at me. "I never thought of you as being Chinese . . . until now."

"What's that got to do with it?" I demanded.

"Why else are you defending her?" Sylvia shrugged. "I thought you were my friend. If she were anyone else, you'd think she was guilty too. But you're taking the side of a perfect stranger against me—just because she's Chinese like you."

I felt . . . well . . . insulted—though I shouldn't have. It wasn't because I thought there was something wrong with China. It's just that I didn't like being called different. "I'm just like you," I insisted.

Despite the recovery of the rabbit's foot, Sylvia was still feeling upset. "You just proved you aren't. Or you'd know who your friends are and who the thieves are."

I had grown up with Sylvia and had known her since second grade. All that time I thought she had considered me her equal. It was a shock to find out that Sylvia might think otherwise now.

I started to turn away. "In America, you get a fair trial no matter what you are."

Behind me, I heard a boy mutter to someone else, "See? She really is a half-breed or she wouldn't be trying to help that thief."

At some other time, I might have ignored the insult; but Sylvia's accusations had already made me feel like I was an outsider. Furious now, I whirled around. "Who said that?"

The nearest boy held up his hands. "It wasn't me."

"Whoever said that was a jerk," Jeff said. "Don't pay him any attention."

However, now that the words had been spoken, they could never be taken back because the damage had been done.

I knew almost everyone there. Quite a few had even gone to elementary school with me. Looking around at the other faces now, I wondered just how many thought that way even though they hadn't said so. Was anyone really my friend? Could I trust anyone again?

"Where are you going, Stacy?" Karen asked in her sad little voice. "Your class is in the other direction."

"I've got to find out something first," I said. Clenching the pen in my fist, I walked away, my strides getting wider and wider and faster and faster. Karen caught up with me.

"I think you need a friend," she said as she panted to keep up with me.

I smiled my thanks at her. Good old Karen was one person I could count on.

As we headed for the lockers of the Dumpster crew, I felt as if I had stepped over the border into a strange new world. It looked like my old one, but when I looked at details, there were things wrong with it.

I kept turning the scene over and over in my mind, and it made me feel ashamed, though there was nothing to be ashamed of. All the way across campus, I felt like kids were whispering and pointing at me like I had escaped from some freak show. Anytime anyone laughed, I even thought it was because of me. With those kinds of suspicions I'd go crazy in no time.

The Dumpster crew was still by their lockers, so I walked straight up to Victor Li. "What's *t'ung chung*?" I repeated the words Hong Ch'un had used for me.

"What?" he asked, puzzled.

When I told Victor again, he nodded his head. "Oh, you mean *t'ung chung*," he said, correcting the tones. "Who said that?"

"Never mind. What does it mean?" I demanded.

Dwight Whang folded his arms smugly. "You think you are one big person. You think you are so good—too good for us."

I was surprised by that. "Whatever gave you that impression?"

"You walk around just like one of these." He waved a hand at some passing white students. "But you are not them. You are not us."

Victor punched Dwight in the arm. "Shut up."

I thrust an arm in between Victor and Dwight. "I want to know," I said to Dwight.

"You don't want to know. Go back to your friends," Victor urged.

I looked at my small, distorted reflection on the lenses of his glasses.

"What does it mean?"

"It means 'mixed seed,'" Dwight translated with satisfaction.

"That's literally," Victor said, trying to be helpful. "But it really means—"

"I know what it means." I lowered my arm. "In English it's half-breed. Is it as much an insult in Chinese as it is in English?"

"More," Victor said. "I'm sorry."

"Aren't we all sorry?" I said, and turned away.

Four

All the rest of that day I walked through the school as if in a dream. Even the harsh ringing of the bell couldn't break the spell.

I thought everyone was turning and snickering. I thought I heard other people speaking my name even when it was just bits of harmless conversation. Half-breed. The word kept repeating over and over in my mind like a squeaking wheel. Half-breed.

All my life I thought I had lived in a safe, warm, secure world where I was just like everyone else, but it had only been my little fantasy. I looked too Chinese. And yet, even if I learned Chinese and the culture, I looked too American. There would always be someone like Dwight to call me a half-breed.

I felt . . . lost.

Classes were a disaster. I went through the motions of paying attention. I'd open my textbooks when everyone else did, and I'd pretend to look at the blackboard, but the writing could have been Sanskrit for all I understood it. Fortunately, I managed to make myself look inconspicuous for most of the day until I hit history. About halfway through the period, I dimly heard Mr. Gibbon say, "Stacy?"

He was standing in front of the blackboard balancing a piece of chalk between his fingertips.

Didn't he realize that this was all a dream? It had to be—because the words I'd heard this morning could not be real. It took an effort to make my lips move. "Yes?"

"I asked you to explain why the Magna Carta is so important," he said impatiently.

Usually he called on me when no one else knew the answer. Most of the time I could provide the information because I liked history. Sometimes in the class it almost seemed as if we were conspirators in a secret joke. But not today.

It didn't surprise me when heads swiveled around to stare. They had just been waiting for an excuse.

"I . . ." I looked at Mr. Gibbon, pleading silently for him to go on to someone else.

However, Mr. Gibbon was like a bulldog that had sunk its teeth into the leg of a tasty mail carrier. "You did it so well in the last test."

I sat mutely, willing myself to be invisible, aware of all the smirks and gleeful looks.

"Come, come." He tapped the chalk against the blackboard.

I felt as if someone had hung a clown's mask over my face. Everyone else had been able to see the mask except for me. And now I was just finding out about it.

"I don't know," I said, hoping to end things quickly.

To my chagrin, Mr. Gibbon left the blackboard and strolled down the aisle between desks. "What's the matter? Don't you feel well?"

I shook my head, trying to make him leave me alone. "I'm fine."

He bent over me solicitously. "Maybe you should see the nurse."

The last thing I wanted was to call even more attention to myself. "I'm fine," I insisted.

"This isn't like you," he said kindly.

I felt something inside me snap. "Please, please, please. Just call on someone else, okay?"

He reared back from that outburst as if I were a crocodile that had just tried to take off his head. "Beverly," he said without looking at her. "Would you care to help out Stacy?"

I felt a moment of panic, thinking that he was

asking Bev to take me to the nurse. However, he only meant that Bev should tell me the answer. As she stumbled through an explanation, he turned away from me mercifully, and so did the others.

It took forever for the final bell to ring, and when it did, I was out of that classroom like a rocket. I already had my pack on my back so I could head straight home.

"Stacy, wait up."

Turning, I saw Karen running toward me. Beyond her I saw the others streaming away from their classrooms. The last thing I wanted was to be caught in the middle of that mob, so I kept on walking.

"Hey," Karen puffed, "are you going home already? I thought you'd be hanging out with Sylvia's bunch."

I really didn't need a second shadow. In some ways, I knew what it was to sit on top of a crate of nitroglycerin. The slightest jar, too deep a breath, the wrong move, and the whole school could blow up. "I've got some things to think over."

Karen rose, sliding her arms into her book bag. "So do I," she said hurriedly. "We can walk together."

"Okay, but *silencio*." I put a finger to my lips.

Karen didn't say anything. She just pulled her fingers across her mouth as if she were zipping it closed. And she was as good as her word, keeping pace beside me as she pushed her bike along.

She broke her vow only when we had finally reached our houses. "Have you reconsidered doing some homework together?" Karen asked.

I hesitated, wondering if I should try to track down Hong Ch'un; but it hadn't been my choice to be her baby-sitter. I'd been drafted. Anyway, she had probably gone home.

"Sure," I said.

As we crossed her lawn, I felt the tall weeds clutch and pull at my ankles. From the porch, I could hear the television thundering behind the door. Karen patted her pockets in a panic. "I think I forgot my keys," she said, and stared at the doorbell.

"It sounds like someone's home," I said.

"Both of my folks are home," she said. "Dad's been laid off and Mom works the swing shift."

I figured she was afraid of waking up her mom. "Would she be asleep now?"

"Oh, no. She's usually up by the afternoon." But Karen continued to gaze at the doorbell.

"Then they won't mind letting us in." I regretted having jabbed the doorbell when I saw the pained expression on Karen's face.

When Mr. Persky jerked the door open, he glowered. "I heard you, I heard you."

Mr. Persky was in a shirt with the collar open and his tie loosened, hanging like a miniature hangman's noose. Though he still wore his suit pants, his feet were bare. At one time, he might have been ruggedly handsome—like Charles Bronson without the mustache—but now he looked more like an old bulldog.

Beyond him, I could see a game roaring away on the television. In front of an easy chair was a TV tray with a microwaved dinner on it.

I'd forgotten how odd the Perskys could be. I tried to smile. "Good afternoon, Mr. Persky."

He ignored me to glare at Karen. "What happened, stupid? Did you forget your keys again?"

Karen never seemed to have much self-esteem, and I could see why, with her father running her down like that. But arguing with Mr. Persky wouldn't do any good.

Karen said nothing and became a hunched-up little figure. Taking her by the shoulders, I shoved her past him, smiling as I followed her. "I hope we didn't disturb you."

Once I was inside, Mr. Persky seemed even more confused—as if he knew how to keep people on his doorstep, but not how to evict them once they were in his house.

He slammed the door behind us. It was funny, but over the excited gabble of the sports announcer, I could hear the sound of violins. "We had to get her those dodo Velcro shoes because she can't tie her own shoelaces."

Mrs. Persky was seated on a sofa about five feet from Mr. Persky's easy chair, but she was gazing intently at a different television set. Both TVs were thundering away at deafening levels.

"Afternoon, Mrs. Persky," I shouted.

Mrs. Persky raised a limp hand and let it flop back on her lap. Neither of Karen's parents were big talkers.

Their house had the same floor plan as mine. Karen led me up the stairs and down a dim hallway toward her bedroom. Once she had banged the door shut behind us, she straightened up and smiled brightly. Karen actually had a pretty smile whenever she could manage one. "It's just nice to have you here," she said, and turned on a little black-and-white TV. Instantly soap-opera-ish violins roared at the same deafening level as her parents' televisions. It was a wonder that the whole family wasn't deaf.

"Can you turn it down a little?" I yelled, and pantomimed turning a dial down.

Karen got the idea and went back to the television and turned it down. As I sat down on her bed, I tried to ask casually, "What do you think of Hong Ch'un?"

Karen scratched the top of her head. "She's not our kind."

"Do you think she's the thief?" I hazarded.

"She's weird enough." Karen wrinkled her forehead into the same puzzled, bulldog expression that her father had. "I thought we were going to do homework together."

"Right," I said. We worked side by side for several hours. When I slammed the last book shut, I stretched luxuriously. "Done."

Karen looked genuinely distressed. "You're not going, are you?"

I felt like I'd just taken a puppy and drop-kicked it sixty yards. However, Karen was the kind of needy friend who was never satisfied. If I spent one whole evening with her, she would want two. I began to remember why I had stopped visiting her. "I have to go home," I said. "I've got to make rice."

I thought she was going to give me a hard time, but she was a good scout this time as I put on my backpack.

Karen escorted me as far as the stairs but seemed afraid to come down where her parents were. Mr. Persky had tuned his TV to the news on Channel 11 and Mrs. Persky's was tuned to the news on Channel 8, so the two announcers seemed to be holding a shouting contest with each other.

"'Bye!" I shouted at them as I crossed the house toward the front door.

But they didn't even bother to answer, and I was glad to leave. Living in Karen's house was like living in a thundercloud.

When I saw the dark sky, I realized that I had lost track of time. I was as much at fault as Mom or Dad about making the time to be together. As I hurried toward home, I couldn't help blaming myself.

And then guilt turned to resentment. Neither Mom's nor Dad's car was in the driveway. I should have known—something had come up to interfere with our family meal.

Well, they'd get an earful when they finally got home and I told them the kind of person they'd stuck me with. And yet even as I planned what to say, I could already hear Mom defending her. Mom was always sticking up for the underdog.

Mom would probably say that if Hong Ch'un was the thief, it wasn't like she had stolen jewelry or the family silver. It was worthless stuff to everyone but the owners.

I wanted to forgive her if she was the thief, but it was just like Mr. Barrows had said: Each bit of stuff she had taken was special to that person—what she had stolen were little bits of the heart. It was too cruel to overlook.

The house was dim and still until I heard tinny gunshot noises wafting down the hallway from the TV in Tai-Paw's room. People shouted at one another angrily in Chinese punctuated by more gunshots. Her door was closed, though, so I went to the answering machine, where the little red light was blinking.

One message was from Cousin Pam—a bad sign because she never called unless she wanted something. She did. The second was from Dad. In the background of his message, I could hear a printer chattering away. "We've got major problems on the assembly line. The robots are going crazy. Wang and I are going to have to miss dinner. Sorry."

I should have known. Something always came up to keep us from doing something as a family.

The next was from Mom: "I'll be running a little late, honey. Got a call from the president of Intel. He wants me to set up training programs for dealing with people of other cultures. Maybe help them redesign their personnel tests."

I let out a whistle. Intel was a major maker of silicon chips, so that sounded like beaucoup bucks.

The other messages were just little things, so I wrote them down on the message pad.

When I had run the answering machine back to the start, I glanced at the rice cooker. Mom had it all set up and ready to go, but I figured Hong Ch'un had gone home to tell her mother that dinner was off.

As for my parents, well, it was another one of their typically busy days—and nights. They should have known that they couldn't escape their usual routines.

Leaving the rice cooker alone, I climbed gratefully up the stairs. The cool shadows of the upper floor closed around me. Slipping into my room, I shut the door and sat on my bed.

I stayed there on my bed, feeling sorry for myself. And all the time there was just one thought inside my mind—one as hot as a potato that you've just taken from a campfire; so hot that you keep tossing it from one hand to the other but you can't let go. And that one thought was: Who am I?

Every answer left me nowhere—as if I had dropped into *The Twilight Zone*. Only there were no commercial breaks and no Rod Serling to come out and tell me when it was over. It was an ongoing episode that I had no script for, and it would roll on endlessly.

I had thought I had fit in as snugly as a center piece in a jigsaw puzzle, when all the time I had been pretending. I had thought I was on top of the world when I had really been on the bottom.

Five

Up in my bedroom, I wound up losing track of time again. My growling stomach told me I needed a snack, but somehow I never got around to it.

When the doorbell rang, I wrapped my arms around myself and tried to huddle into a ball. When the doorbell sounded again, I began to feel angry.

I still didn't want to leave my room, but if I didn't go, Tai-Paw would have to. So, reluctantly, I stepped out into the hallway. I took my time, hoping that whoever our visitor was would go away. However, our caller persisted in punching the doorbell.

All kinds of possibilities tumbled through my mind, but I wasn't prepared for the sight of a strange cabdriver. "Yes, what is it?" I asked him.

"Thank God you can speak English," he said. "Maybe you can interpret for me."

When Mrs. Wang stepped around him, she looked relieved. "Stay-cee?" She rattled off a lot of Chinese at me as she waved a twenty-dollar bill in one hand and a pink, horseshoe-decorated wallet in the other. Beyond them in the street was a yellow taxicab with its motor running.

The cabby ran a hand through what remained of his hair. "I keep trying to explain to her that I don't have no change for a twenty."

Mrs. Wang tried to thrust the twenty-dollar bill into the driver's hand. Though neither of us could understand her Chinese, her tone made it plain that she was getting exasperated.

"How much is it?" I asked.

"Well, the fare was four eighty," the cabdriver said. "But there's always room for some gratitude."

"I'll get it." I darted into the kitchen and went to the cabinet where Mom kept the emergency money. I got six dollars and brought it back.

The driver grunted his thanks and beat a quick retreat to his taxi. As he passed, Mrs. Wang continued to wave her twenty-dollar bill—first at him, and then, when he had gotten into his cab, she tried to give it to me.

Fortunately, Tai-Paw had come out of her room. She said something in Cantonese, but Mrs. Wang didn't understand. So Tai-Paw grasped Mrs. Wang's wrist and forced it firmly back toward the horseshoe-patterned wallet.

Under other circumstances, I would have thought it was pretty funny to see the two wrestling each other. I'd seen Mom battle her cousins to pick up the restaurant tab. Once, she actually had torn the check in half when she pulled one way and her cousin Pam pulled the other. In fact, I was surprised that one of those normally polite, well-dressed, professional women had not dislocated a shoulder. When I asked Mom about that afterward, she explained to me that it was a matter of face, or pride.

At the beginning of the struggle, I would have given you odds on Mrs. Wang, who was younger and stronger, but Tai-Paw was the wily veteran of many such fights and had all sorts of tricks up her sleeve. Like Godzilla battling Mega-Godzilla, she easily bested Mrs. Wang. The upshot was that Mrs. Wang, complaining all the while, tucked her twenty-dollar bill back into her wallet.

Once the preliminary match was finished, I didn't know what else to do except step back into the house and gesture Mrs. Wang inside. "Won't you come in?" I asked politely.

As she followed Tai-Paw into the house, Mrs. Wang asked us, "Ching-Jiu?" And once she was inside, she called out in a loud, hopeful voice, "Hong Ch'un?" She turned to her left and shouted again.

When I touched her arm, Mrs. Wang whirled around. "Didn't Hong Ch'un come home yet?"

Mrs. Wang's anxious, frightened words flew right by me. Shutting the door, Tai-Paw said something in Cantonese, but it did nothing to calm Mrs. Wang, who did not understand.

Leaving them for a moment, I went into Dad's study. I knew Dad would kill me if he found out, but this was an emergency. The room was typical Dad, with shelves of sturdy, practical steel; a heavy desk made out of thick slabs of pine, which Granddad had made for him when he went into high school; and over the desk, for purposes of meditation, a picture of Dwight Clark making "The Catch" that beat the Cowboys to get the 49ers into their first Super Bowl. And next to it was a picture of Mom and her father, Barney.

I switched on the old fluorescent light. I didn't know the vintage, but it probably dated back to Dad's high school years as well—Dad was too sentimental to throw away anything. Next to it was a square photo from one of those cheap cameras. The pictures were fading, but I could see Dad when he had been in junior high with a buzz to end all buzz haircuts and showing his already plump shape. Someday soon, I told myself, we ought to get the photo reshot before the colors disappeared altogether.

Dad's Rolodex was right by the computer modem, and I began flipping through the cards, but I couldn't find Mr. Wang. It took me a moment to realize that Dad would've stopped updating his Rolodex by hand once he'd gotten a computer.

I snapped on his Mac and got the mouse. After a minute I found what I wanted; it listed Mr. Wang's office number. The phone pad sang as I punched the buttons, and Mr. Wang answered. "Yes?" He sounded very harried and impatient.

I knew that he was working late on the same project as Dad. "Mr. Wang, we have your wife here and we're not sure what the problem is. Could you speak to her?"

"Of course. Please put her on," Mr. Wang said, sounding a little worried.

Going to the study doorway, I shouted down the hallway. "Tai-Paw, would you bring Mrs. Wang here? I have her husband on the line. Maybe he can interpret."

The next moment, Tai-Paw shepherded Mrs. Wang into the hallway. I motioned her into the study, and when she picked up the phone she seemed more upset to hear it was her husband.

As she spoke into the phone, her voice had a pleading tone—as if she were trying to find excuses for her daughter. But after a moment, she beckoned me to the phone.

When I took the receiver, Mr. Wang was very stiff. Whatever his wife had said hadn't worked. "My wife says that Hong Ch'un is not yet home. Is she there?"

"No," I said. "And I don't know where she is."

Mr. Wang sounded as if he didn't quite believe me. "Where is she?"

I glanced at the uncomfortable Mrs. Wang and then at Tai-Paw. "She stole a pen and a toy and a rabbit's foot." I felt stupid accusing anyone of those thefts.

"Why would my daughter take those silly things?" Mr. Wang demanded.

His tone annoyed me. "I don't know, sir, but we found them in her backpack."

After a long pause, he exhaled in a long, slow sigh. "I'm sorry." I suspected it cost him a great deal to apologize. "I don't understand how Hong Ch'un could do that to her schoolmates." Mr. Wang sounded as if he was ready to cry. "We were so worried that Hong Ch'un would not adjust. She had so many friends back home. She was so popular. It was hard to come to a new country where she knows no one."

I wanted to ask him why she had insulted me by calling me a mixed seed. But the words wouldn't come to my tongue.

Mr. Wang was simply bewildered now. "Because Almaden only has one junior high, we knew you would be together. We hoped you and she would become good friends. Please put my wife back on," he asked.

Mrs. Wang took it when I held it out to her. She kept beginning sentences but breaking off in mid word, as if Mr. Wang had interrupted her. Every now and then, she would try a stammering interjection, but Mr. Wang must have been reading her the riot act.

Finally Tai-Paw liberated the receiver from the unhappy Mrs. Wang and said decisively, "Mr. Wang. This is Stacy's grandmother. How are you?" She did not wait for a response but cut right to the heart of the matter. "I know there must be some reasonable explanation for what happened. But in the meantime we have to find Hong Ch'un. Do you have any idea where she could be?"

After a moment, she put Mrs. Wang back on. I suppose Mr. Wang must have come to his senses because Mrs. Wang actually got to discuss the matter with him.

When they were done, Mrs. Wang gave Tai-Paw the phone. Tai-Paw nodded her head as she listened. "No, of course, we can get up there. Don't worry. We'll find her if she's there." When she had handed the receiver back to Mrs. Wang, she said to me, "Mr. Wang said that he has a cousin who works in Chinatown. He believes Hong Ch'un may have tried to go up there.

But his wife will go home and wait, just in case Hong Ch'un comes back."

As Mrs. Wang nodded her head to Mr. Wang's instructions, Tai-Paw told me an address to write down. I had to keep repeating it to myself because all the pencils in Dad's study were broken and all the pens seemed to be dried out. If Dad couldn't type it into a computer, it wasn't worth writing down.

Finally, though, I recovered a stub of a pencil from a desk drawer and quickly jotted the address on a notepad. As soon as I was finished, Tai-Paw had me read it back to her. "That sounds right," she said with a nod. "When Mrs. Wang is finished, please call a taxicab for me."

My eyes grew big. "You can't take a cab all the way up to San Francisco. That would cost a fortune."

She glanced sympathetically at Hong Ch'un's mother. "I only want to drop Mrs. Wang off. Then I will take a train or a bus to San Francisco."

"How do you know she's even there?" I asked.

"It's the only other place where she knows someone," Tai-Paw said. "And Mr. Wang had given her some money to buy you a treat."

I was still alarmed at the idea of her going off on her own, but I had never seen her so determined. "You can't go up to the City alone."

Tai-paw folded up the address. I suppose she would ask someone to read the address back to her if she forgot it. "I know my way around. Hong Ch'un does not. Think of how lonesome she must be."

I didn't relish the idea of trying to rescue someone who considered me less than human—and who'd tried to shift the blame on me, to boot. "She's a thief. She brought it on herself."

"She's all alone," Tai-Paw pointed out.

It seemed like the ultimate test to forgive in spite of the hurt and rescue my enemy. Still, no matter what Hong Ch'un had said or done to me, I couldn't let Tai-Paw go on that journey by herself. I had to be as selfless as she was. "I'll go too," I said.

At that moment, Mom's irritated shout echoed through the house. "Stacy, where are you?"

I wondered what I had done wrong now. "I'm in Dad's study," I called.

In her lightning-bolt mode, Mom kept talking as she flew up the hallway toward us. "I spoke to your dad this afternoon. He said that you were rude to Hong Ch'un this morning."

"Dad said that about me?" I asked in surprise.

"No, I wormed it out of him," Mom said. She was good at prying the facts out of Dad when he tried to cover for me.

Tai-Paw pulled me behind her as Mom burst through the doorway. "Can you take Mrs. Wang home right now?" she asked quickly. "Otherwise we will drop her off."

Remembering her manners, Mom smiled a brief hello at Mrs. Wang and then looked back at Tai-Paw. "Drop her off? Where are you going?"

Tai-Paw motioned toward me. "Hong Ch'un stole some things at school—perhaps as a prank—and now she's run away."

I picked up the phone after Mrs. Wang had hung up. "That's right."

Mom stared down at me. "Really?"

Cradling the phone between my chin and shoulder, I punched in 411. "I saw that she had them."

"What did you actually see, Stacy?" Mom asked intently.

"Well," I said slowly, trying to remember as the phone rang. "I heard a clink and saw the pen by her foot. And the other two things were in her bag."

"Maybe it was some form of retaliation for your rudeness this morning," Mom suggested.

"Why do you always assume it's my fault?" I demanded. "Maybe she was the first one to be rude."

"You were her host," Mom snapped. "You were supposed to be patient."

A machine at the other end of the line announced that I was on hold. "Even when she called me a half-breed?" I asked.

Mom and Tai-Paw both sucked in their breaths. "She did?" Mom asked.

I could feel my cheeks flushing. Even now, I found it terribly embarrassing. I repeated the Chinese phrase for them and then added, "Trying to make us stick together was like mixing oil and water."

"I'm sorry." Mom put an arm around me and gave me a hug. "We've tried to protect you from that sort of thing."

Mrs. Wang had heard the phrase and asked a question in Mandarin. And when Mom made a halting explanation in the same dialect, Mrs. Wang put a shocked hand to her mouth and then rushed over to me and began talking urgently.

"She's apologizing," Mom interpreted for me.

I forced myself to smile and said, "It's okay" over and over—though I was still hurting inside.

In the meantime, Tai-Paw was wrestling with herself. "Well, we can't correct her ignorance if she's missing."

Mom played with her charm bracelet. She had clearly lost her taste for playing host to the Wangs. "Why don't you leave it to the police?"

"They will not begin to look for forty-eight hours. I

saw it on *The Streets of San Francisco*," Tai-Paw said. "I have to find her. It's what her own grandmother would do. Think of how you would feel if you were her."

No matter what I thought of Hong Ch'un, I had to admit that Tai-Paw was right. "Even if I don't care much for her opinions, we can't let her wander around strange streets."

At that moment, the operator came on and identified herself. "City?" she inquired.

I told her and then asked, "May I have the number of Yellow Cab?"

Mom abruptly pushed the receiver button down, cutting off the call. "I'll take you to San Francisco."

"But you're always so busy," Tai-Paw said. "You never have time to go to San Francisco."

Mom managed a little grin. "I say that a lot, don't I?"

"You're a very important person," Tai-Paw said.

Mom contemplated the picture of her father. "When you say that, I think of Barney—especially when the dice were hot. He'd buy a cigar—the biggest but not necessarily the best—and for a couple of days it'd be free eats and drinks for everybody."

"Granddad gambled?" I asked in surprise. I always wondered why she had lived with Tai-Paw in Chinatown rather than with her father, but whenever I had asked her, she had put me off.

Mom pressed her lips together in a thin, tight smile as if there was an old, secret pain. "I guess you're old enough now to know. Gambling was his disease. But don't tell anyone."

Tai-Paw gave Mom a hug. "And he stopped for your sake."

"But not the big talking." Embarrassed, Mom fingered the little owl charm. Tai-Paw had asked her friend Mr. Jeh to copy it from an heirloom she used to own, and she had given it as a present to Mom. I thought it was a little clunky looking, but it was Mom's favorite piece of jewelry.

"At least I had you looking out for me in Chinatown. I hope Mr. Wang's cousin is there." Suddenly she sighed as she shook her head. "Well, the president of Intel will just have to understand if I have to postpone my meeting tomorrow because I'm not prepared."

"But it's important, Mom," I said, offering her an out.

Mom seemed to draw strength from the charm and the woman who gave it to her. "Sometimes there are more important things."

Six

When Mom tried to postpone the meeting, though, I thought she was going to have to change her mind again. Her face got red and angry. She kept trying to interject something, but the person on the other end of the line wouldn't stop talking. For a while, she toyed with the owl charm; finally she just announced, "I'm sorry. This is more important." And she slammed the receiver back on the cradle.

"Are you sure?" Tai-Paw asked.

Mom managed a smile. "Of course," she said to her grandmother, and then to me, "Stacy, will you get Mrs. Wang's address?"

I had to go into Dad's computer again. The funny thing was that it wasn't any place I had heard of. It made me wonder again about the contrast between Hong Ch'un's life in China and here.

Turning off the Mac, I went outside with Mrs.

Wang and Tai-Paw (who had tied a bandanna on her head). Mom was outside hastily cleaning out her car, which consisted of transferring everything from the floor to the trunk.

I helped Tai-Paw into the backseat while Mrs. Wang got in from the other side.

The car rocked as Mom slammed the trunk lid down, then I gave her the address. When she read the note, she frowned. "You're kidding," she said.

I walked around to the passenger side of the front seat. "No, that's the place. Know where it is?"

"If it's where I think it is, keep the buttons down," Mom warned.

That was the first inkling I had that the real state of the Wangs might not be as glorious as Hong Ch'un liked to pretend. I remembered how she had bragged to me. Coming here must have been a real letdown.

Mom drove us across El Camino, where the neon-lit fast-food places were. The houses began to look older and smaller and more run-down. Here and there you could spot some place that was being kept meticulously neat, but most of them were getting seedy, and a lot of them began to have fences and even "Beware of the Dog" signs.

When we rolled into a street filled with bail bondspeople and pawnshops, I turned to Mom. "Where are we going?"

"This is the place you gave me." She pointed at a street sign.

As we swung beneath it, I understood why Hong Ch'un felt America was such a letdown. Outside the apartment buildings there were a lot of scruffy types holding up the walls; and they eyed us as we rolled on past. There was an old movie theater that probably hadn't been used in years, except as a urinal by the drunks.

Finally we saw the number on a skid-row tenement.

"Here, here," Mrs. Wang said from behind us. She pointed at a set of windows on the first floor. What furniture I could see didn't match—as if it had all come from Salvation Army—though Mrs. Wang had tried to cover over the frayed parts with patches of bright silk.

Though she had hardly said more than ten words at our place, she chattered on now—as if she were more comfortable on her own turf. Mom got out with her. "I'll see you to the door."

Getting her keys out of her coat, Mrs. Wang unlocked the door. As she stepped through the doorway, she turned and grabbed Mom's arm.

"Don't worry," Mom assured her. "We'll find your daughter."

Mrs. Wang pulled Mom through the front door, though, leaving Tai-Paw and me alone.

As the front door closed behind them, I wondered what it had been like for Tai-Paw when she had first come to America. Funny that I had never thought to ask Tai-Paw about her earlier years.

When I did ask her, she was settling into the rear seat, which she now had to herself. "Very, very scary."

I leaned my arm on top of the seat. "Did you ever want to go back?"

Tai-Paw leaned her head back against the seat. "Only in the last few years, when my hip started to get worse." She made a little face the way she always did when she mentioned Great-Uncle Philip. "And your Uncle Philip wanted me to go to an old folks' home. Me, with those old relics! So I told him to leave me alone. I'd make out on my own. He didn't have to worry anymore about my spoiling the fancy decor."

Tai-Paw had bounced around from one relative to another until Mom talked Dad into giving up their own master bedroom.

As I remembered the arguments between Mom and Dad, I picked at some loose threads on the seat cover. "Are you sorry you moved in with us?"

"I was scared at first," she admitted, "because I didn't know what to expect."

Dad hadn't exactly been overjoyed at having his life overturned either. The man who has to have everything laid out exactly right on his desk doesn't like to change his life much.

"It helped that your father was a 'pussycat,'" Tai-Paw said.

"That's because you always take his side rather than Mom's," I said. That's how Tai-Paw had quickly won him over. Now he wouldn't have parted with her for any amount of money.

Mom came bustling back out of the building. As she opened the door, she showed us a photo. "Mrs. Wang wanted me to take a picture of Hong Ch'un."

I thought it would make a good mug shot, but I refrained from saying so.

As Mom slid back behind the wheel, she announced, "Next stop, San Francisco."

Since I had a professional shrink next to me, I thought I might as well take advantage of it.

"Why do you think someone would steal things that aren't worth much?" I asked. "It's the sentimental value that makes them important. Whoever the thief is, he or she seems more mean than greedy."

"Maybe the thief can't help it." Mom changed lanes. "It might be a kleptomaniac acting on impulse."

I settled against the seat. "Like a shoplifter?"

Mom ignored me while she tried to merge into the traffic on the freeway. I wished I had her ability to focus on one thing at a time. When she had successfully joined the flow, she corrected me. "That word gets misapplied to petty thieves. No, I'm talking about a true kleptomaniac. Someone who's searching for a number of things: security, absolution for their crimes, or even some way to create self-esteem."

Sometimes talking to Mom made me more confused—which is why I had given up a while back. "So kleptomaniacs try to steal those things from people who have them?"

With a jab of her thumb, Mom turned on the traffic news, but I saw that she had the same pained look on her face that I got when Dad asked a dumb question about a musical superstar. "Symbolically, yes."

When I saw that expression on her face, I felt myself grow angry. It's funny, but separately Mom and I could get along with everyone—just not with each other. She always acted like I was a failure when I didn't follow her right away. "Forget it," I snapped.

Mom studied me for a moment and then consciously softened her voice when she spoke—as if she was determined to make up for what Hong Ch'un had said. "I'm sorry, dear. Many compulsive thieves feel cheated in the first place because they never got those things that other people did. But they're scared of expressing it openly. So instead, they steal them secretly—love, pride, beauty. They may even feel like they have the *right* to take them."

My mind inevitably turned back to Hong Ch'un. "And they might even be defensive about it. Even self-righteous."

"And very hungry," Tai-Paw said.

"What do you mean by that?" I asked.

Tai-Paw glanced at me uncomfortably. "I was thinking about another thief."

"What other thief?" I asked curiously.

"You don't want to know," she said defensively.

I was a little hurt by her reaction. She made it sound as if I treated her like furniture—though now that I thought of it, I could not remember a time I had asked her for advice. "But I want to."

Tai-Paw studied me as if she were trying to decide if I was mocking her. I wondered if that was the reason why she grew so quiet when my friends were around. She really did become like a stick of furniture then. "It's a story, and you're too old for stories."

"Who said?" I demanded.

Tai-Paw nudged me. "You did."

First Karen and now Tai-Paw. I guess the SS *Stacy* barreled along like an ocean liner, overturning any little boat that got in her way. "I like your stories."

"When you were small." Tai-Paw watched a red Porsche roar past. "But then you got bigger."

When I had been little, I used to be in Tai-Paw's room all the time, and her television would be dark. While she told me stories, as I recall, I'd be lying down on her narrow bed and smelling her scent in the quilts. It was a strong, musky scent that was not unpleasant— just exotic. When I was older, I realized that it was a compound of her herbal ointments and the incense she burned for her gods sitting on her bureau.

To my chagrin, I couldn't recall the last time I had done that. And now her TV was almost always on. I had thought it was because Mom had gotten Tai-Paw her own cable hook-up so she could watch the Chinese-language stations, but maybe she watched television because she had nothing else to do.

"I'm sorry, Tai-Paw."

Tai-Paw smiled. "Don't be. You grow up and you grow away. I saw it with my children and my grand-children and now my great-grandchildren."

"I'd really like to know what you meant." I glanced at Mom, but she was busy listening to the news. Lowering my voice, I said, "I can't talk to Mom. Ask her a question and I could get a lecture from Psych 101."

Deciding to get comfortable, Tai-Paw kicked off one of her shoes. "The Thief of Hearts could tell you that you seldom get what you want."

I felt little and young again—when Mom and Dad

took care of all the major troubles. In those days, my only problem had been making Jeff stop sticking his tongue out at me, though at the time it had seemed major enough. "Who's the Thief of Hearts?"

Tai-Paw kicked off her other shoe. "You wouldn't want to know. It's too sad. My mother-in-law told it to us when my husband announced his decision to leave China."

"Please tell me about the Thief of Hearts."

She rubbed her feet together in a clumsy massage. "Are you sure?"

When I prompted her again, she began. "Once there was a careless young man. He lived in the cozy little village of Pine Tree upon a hillside overlooking a river. It was a nice place, but guess what."

I picked up my cue. "What?"

Tai-Paw drew her eyebrows together. "There are always some who can't be satisfied." She watched the cars flash by the window for a moment.

The young man and his friends thought they were cleverer than they were. Worse, they were always trying to prove it by pulling all sorts of practical jokes on the other villagers. His family tried to get him to stop, but he would soon become bored and begin his old tricks again.

One day, though, he played one prank too many. The villagers became so angry that he and his friends had to run off into the woods.

Among the tall, dark trees, they quickly became separated. Alone, the young man wandered through the forest until he came to a hill, and in the hill was a grotto. Around a pool were columns of stone like veils of rock, and others like ribbons. Pink and brown and all kinds of colors.

By the pool, he saw the loveliest girl he had ever seen, and he fell instantly in love with her. "What's your name?" he asked.

"Don't be tiresome," she said, and ran deeper into the cavern.

And the young man followed her between the stone pillars and odd-shaped rocks.

"How did he see?" I asked.

"Light came from the rocks," Tai-Paw said. "And just when he thought he was going to catch her, suddenly a huge, blue-skinned ogre appeared in front of him. 'Who are you?' he demanded."

The young man would have run, but the ogre seized his collar and hoisted him off the ground.

"I s-s-saw a girl," the young man stammered. "So I followed her. But my intentions were purely honorable. I wanted to know her name so I could send a matchmaker around."

The young man prepared to be torn limb from limb, but instead the ogre threw back his head and roared with laughter. "And what say you, daughter? Will I have him as my son-in-law or as my dinner?"

The girl appeared at the ogre's side. When she smiled, she was even lovelier. "I'll marry him."

The ogre declared, "Then marry him you shall." And he set the young man upon his feet.

Dazed, the young man let himself be led deep inside the cave to a palace where the ogre and his family lived.

At the doors, the ogre told them to kneel and worship heaven and earth together. Eagerly the young man got down on his knees, but when he looked toward the ogre's eldest daughter, she vanished.

The ogre roared with laughter. "Ho, ho, ho! What's the use of giving you my daughter if you can't keep her?" And he stepped into the palace.

Cautiously the young man followed the ogre. There, in a large banquet chamber, he found the ogre's eldest daughter getting everything ready for a feast.

The young man was so upset that he forgot to whom he was speaking. Running up, he grabbed the ogre's arm. "Is this all just an elaborate joke?"

The ogre shook him off as easily as if he were a flea. "And what say you, daughter? Shall I have him as a son-in-law or as dinner?"

"I won't have a fool." And the daughter explained to the young man, "If you can steal my heart, I will not be able to disappear."

"But to cut you open would be to kill you," the anguished man said, "and I could never do that."

"Fool," the ogre's daughter said, "my heart is not in my body but outside."

"And where is that?" the young man asked.

"You must find the secret," the ogre told him. "And you must do that in a month, or I really *will* have you for dinner. By then, you should be good and fattened up for eating."

"Then I will find and take your heart," the young man promised, "for I can think of no one but you."

So he thought and thought, but day after

day passed and he could not come up with a clever enough plan. Finally, on the day before he was to be eaten, he came up with an idea. Though the walls of the palace were of stone, the furniture was of wood, and there were costly screens and paintings and rugs. After he had broken up a chair, he started a fire.

As the smoke filled room after room, the ogre's family and servants ran about trying to save the most precious things. However, the young man kept his eye on the daughter and saw that she darted to a cabinet and unlocked it. Inside the cabinet was a jar, and inside the jar was her heart. Picking up the jar, she ran out of the smoke-filled palace. While everyone else fled, the clever young man examined the cabinet; one side was big enough to hide in. So he got inside and squeezed onto a bottom shelf.

A servant found the fire that the young man had started and put it out. Then he went outside to tell the ogre, who became very angry. "That little sneak. He's trying to cheat us out of our dinner. He started the fire to hide his escape. It's not very sporting of him."

And the ogre and his servants set off to chase the young man and drag him back. However, the daughter went back to the cabinet first. She did not see the young man, who was hidden in the back behind quilts and bolts of cloth.

After she had locked the doors again, he managed to grab the jar. The ogre did not return until hours later. "Next time, I'll eat the fool right away. No more playing with my dinner."

He was surprised when he heard a tapping sound from inside one of the cabinets. Going to the doors, he broke them open. Out stepped the young man with the jar. "I've stolen your daughter's heart," he said.

Now the eldest daughter was just as shocked as her father was. "But I don't really want to be your wife."

The ogre looked at her mournfully. "We've given him our word."

"But he's a . . . a human," the horrified daughter insisted. "And our children would be half of our world and half of that other."

"But," I said to Tai-Paw, "if he stole her heart, why doesn't she love him?"

"You're thinking like an American." Tai-Paw patted my arm. "The old-time Chinese say the heart rules the body. All your *thoughts* come from there, not your feelings." She scratched her cheek. "It's more like what Americans call the mind."

I usually avoided trying to talk about Chinese stuff with Tai-Paw because sometimes it was as hard to understand as Mom or Dad's shoptalk. However, it intrigued me how two cultures could look in such a different way at what's basically a big muscle. So for once I was willing to try to understand Tai-Paw. "But a mind is a brain."

"In the old days, the Chinese used to say the head is where all the . . . the life energy is." She tapped her own forehead in illustration. "That's why the god of long life has such a big head. No, the heart has seven eyes. If the eyes are clear, everything is okay."

Sometimes when she gave an explanation, she raised more questions than she answered—though when I was small that hadn't kept me from asking for stories. I had simply ignored the stuff I didn't understand—just like I had with Dad's science fiction shows. Now I was beginning to suspect that I'd missed some interesting things.

"So anyway, what happened to the Thief of Hearts?" I asked.

"Well, the ogre scolded and the young man begged," Tai-Paw continued, "but they could not get her to change her mind."

So the young man sadly handed the jar back to her. "Then take back your heart as you've taken back your word."

Ashamed, the ogre would have loaded him down with gold and jewels, but the young man refused. He left the cavern and wandered through the woods until he found the river. "This will take me to Pine Tree."

He walked along the riverbank until he came to the edge of the wood. "I must have taken a wrong turn somewhere. This isn't my village." He found himself standing before a city.

So he went to a soldier guarding the gates and asked directions to Pine Tree. The man looked at him as if he were a fool and laughed. "This city *is* Pine Tree."

"But Pine Tree is only a little village," the young man said.

"It was a long time ago, but now it's grown into an important city," the soldier said.

"How long ago?" the young man asked.

And when the soldier told him, he realized he had been away for centuries. His family and friends were all gone. He cursed himself and began to weep. "I may have stolen her heart, but someone has stolen my world."

So in despair he fled back to the woods and sat beneath a tree. With nothing left to live for, he wasted away and died.

One day a passing peddler saw the remains of the thief. Taking pity on the poor boy, he dug a hole and started to gather the bones to put into the hole. However, among the bones he found a heart of deep green jade. "Now this is a good deed that will be repaid," he said.

Then a strange thing happened, for the jade heart began to sing. It sang of lost kingdoms and worlds, of lost loves and lost dreams until the peddler wept.

Blessing his good fortune, he set the heart aside and buried the bones and said a hopeful prayer for the thief's ghost.

Then, putting the jade heart into his basket, he set out again. He had not gone very far before he came across the ogre, who stole everything he had, including the singing heart.

As the ogre's family went through the loot, they took delight in each item. "What's in here?" asked his daughter. When she took out the jade heart, it burst into such a sad love song that she and all the others began to weep.

"Throw it away," the sobbing ogre said, "before we all drown in our tears."

His daughter, though, recognized the voice. "It sounds like that human who tried to steal my heart."

The ogre sniffled. "This must be all that's left of the fellow."

And the ogre's daughter was sorry then that she had refused him. "But now it's too late," she said. "I must keep it."

The ogre waved for her to go. "Then don't let me hear it, or I'll bawl night and day."

"I shall put it beside my own heart," the daughter said.

She took it to her room, but she had no sooner placed the thief's precious heart beside her own than the jade heart began the saddest song of all. It sang of unrequited love and lost hope until she burst into tears.

"He has truly stolen my heart now," she mourned. "For now all I can think about is what I have lost."

Tai-Paw snapped her purse open. "And do you know what happened next?"

"The ogre made him come to life again?" I suggested.

"No." Tai-Paw fished around until she found a roll

of Lifesavers. However, her rheumatism had stiffened her fingers so that she had trouble taking one from the roll. "When the jade heart had sung the last notes, it broke into a thousand pieces, and the Thief of Hearts was no more."

I took the Lifesavers and pulled the first one off. It was a pineapple-flavored one. "I thought you were kidding about the story being sad."

With a shake of her head she pointed to a red stripe on the wrapper. "That thief might have been just as miserable if he had stayed at home. This way he had a chance to hope, and when he first stole the daughter's heart, he was happy for a little while."

I peeled back the wrapper until I found a red one. "I still think you should have changed the ending."

She took it with a shrug. "You're older now. I don't have to."

"I'm not that old." I put the pineapple one in my mouth.

Carefully rewrapping the Lifesavers, Tai-Paw restored them to her purse. "But you know a lot of things. Like wanting isn't the same as having. I saw it all the time in Chinatown. I see it down here. Only in Almaden, people want lots more."

Tai-Paw knew as much as Mom. She just didn't use all the fancy words. In a way, Jeff's toy and Sylvia's lucky charm had a little bit of their souls tied up in them—love for Jeff and confidence for Sylvia—and yet today I had found out there were worse thefts. "I think the Thief of Hearts died because he had missed a whole world—not just the ogre's daughter. What she had stolen from him was a lot worse than anything he stole from her."

Tai-Paw jumped when a dead leaf rattled in the car's ventilation system. She had an uneasy truce with machines at best. "There are always new worlds."

I thought of how lost I had felt when I had been called a half-breed. I wondered if the thief had felt the same way when he had stumbled back to his village. "How do you find them?"

Tai-Paw frowned as if she did not understand the question at all. "You look for them."

She knew who she was. I envied her confidence, but I was like the Thief of Hearts, wandering alone through the world.

Seven

When we rounded Hospital Curve on 101, we saw the City. The windows of the hotels and office buildings twinkled like star-filled trees, and at their roots, boxlike apartments and houses lay scattered.

I held my breath the way I always did. Part of it was just the view and part of it was the feeling that I was returning to the home country. Even though I had never spent more than half a day in San Francisco, I had heard so much about it from Mom and Tai-Paw that I thought I knew it.

Mom scanned the skyline critically over the river of red taillights. "Every year the skyline gets taller."

As eager as a kid, Tai-Paw craned to get a better look. "I can't even see Chinatown," she complained.

"When was the last time you were there?" I asked her.

That question set her back. It took Mom and her a

few minutes to work out that it was something like eight years.

Tai-Paw tapped the sides of her eyes. "But in here I can see Chinatown just as fresh as ever."

I glanced at Mom. "When was the last time you saw it, Mom?"

As Mom swung off the freeway, she pursed her lips. "I think it was your fifth birthday, when we took you up to the City."

"I remember," I said. At that age, it had all looked strange and funny and colorful—just like a movie set.

"But we only took you along Grant Avenue. Tonight you're going to see the real Chinatown," Mom promised as we joined the stream of cars flowing off the freeway.

San Francisco itself was so different from where we lived. In Almaden everything was spread out and flat. Here, all the buildings were jammed together as they followed the slopes of the hills. A few places had lawns, but they were just scraps.

Each block we drove seemed to get steeper and higher, so it unnerved me when Mom took her eyes off the road long enough to glance at an apartment house. "The Gibraltar is closed."

"Good," Tai-Paw grunted. "I didn't like the way the manager thought you were a thief."

"He thought all the newspaper carriers were thieves," Mom said.

I turned in surprise. "You delivered newspapers?"

Mom glanced at me uncomfortably as if she expected me to make fun of her. "Things weren't always easy."

I let out a whistle. Coming from someplace as level as Almaden, I could never quite get used to hills—let alone think of carrying a load of newspapers. "You walked these hills, Mom?"

When I didn't make fun of her, she relaxed a little and nodded her head as she swung the car down another street. "With two sacks of newspapers. One in front and one in back."

Climbing these hills would have been bad enough without having to carry a heavy load. I glanced at her suit trousers. "You must have had legs like a mountain goat."

We laughed. "In those days you wouldn't have wanted me to kick you."

Wanting to know more, I asked, "What else did you do? I know Dad lived all over the world on Army bases, but I know hardly anything about you."

Mom clammed up as if she had revealed too much. "It's all old news. You'd just laugh."

I was hurt. "You make me feel like I'm a monster."

Mom hesitated and then tried to make it into a joke. "Are you trying to turn me into one of those mothers who tell their daughters that they used to have to walk ten miles through the snow?"

I gripped the dashboard in frustration. "I just want to know. You'd almost think you were ashamed."

The soft light deepened as we drew directly underneath a streetlamp. "I'm not ashamed of anything," Mom snapped. "You never wanted to listen to me in the past."

"Not if the history came with a lecture," I explained.

Tai-Paw sat up so suddenly that I thought something was wrong, but she had pressed her face against the car window. "Look!" she said, surprised. "That store sells Chinese music." Posters for Chinese singers covered the windows. "What's it doing way up here?"

"Chinatown's spilled out over its borders." The car lurched as Mom screeched to a halt for an elderly Chinese woman carrying a baby in a cloth sling. "And so have the pedestrians."

"In one of the library books," I said, "it said that the Chinese kept living in Chinatown because they wanted to."

Mom made a rude noise. "They wanted to move out, but a lot of places outside Chinatown wouldn't rent to them. But the Fair Housing laws changed that. My friend Talia Chew was the first. She moved out by the ocean. Now it's almost all Chinese out there."

"So many more people came in," Tai-Paw said, "that Chinatown would have exploded otherwise."

"They changed the immigration laws," Mom explained to me, "so the quotas were finally fair."

Tai-Paw gripped the back of my seat. "And so many families could finally get back together. My friend Mr. Jeh was finally able to bring over his children after thirty years."

"What about Mrs. Jeh?" I asked.

"She died in the meantime," Tai-Paw sighed. "So many sad stories like that."

As we topped the hill, I caught peeks of the old Chinatown through the tall stone canyons: green-and-red-colored roofs with corners that curled like frog tongues and signs with Chinese words that twisted like snakes. And farther down the hill, skyscrapers rose in shiny silver-and-black slabs. It was almost as if someone had rolled exotic toy blocks down a hill until they had come up hard against a wall of steel and glass.

Compared to the suburbs, Chinatown seemed as strange as a slice of the moon. I felt just like the Thief of Hearts when he had entered the ogre's cavern, but to Tai-Paw it was home.

"And Chinatown stays Chinatown," Tai-Paw murmured, and I found myself wondering if Almaden seemed just as strange to her. I was embarrassed that I had never thought about asking her.

"We've got to take Stacy for the grand tour some-day and show her our old haunts," Mom suggested to Tai-Paw.

Tai-Paw immediately warmed to the notion. "We have to go with her to Sarah's for ginger ice cream."

"Ginger?" I asked skeptically.

Tai-Paw tapped me on the shoulder. "You'll love it." And she leaned over the front seat to talk to Mom. "Remember the *gwoon foon* at the Celestial?"

"That's barbecued pork and all kinds of good stuff rolled up and then cut into pieces," Mom told me. "I used to get it by the pint and then eat it on my way to the newspaper pickup point."

"Stop," Tai-Paw moaned. "You're making me hungry."

Mom smacked her lips. "Why don't I jump out and get some?"

I looked dubiously around at the crowded streets. The cars were jammed so close to one another that they looked as if they were glued together. "Good luck finding parking."

"You could run in and get it while I double-park," Mom suggested.

I found myself panicking at the idea. "Me? I can't speak Chinese."

"You just need to practice the words," Mom said,

and repeated them for me while her other hand dug around in her purse for her wallet.

I dutifully practiced the phrases as we drove along, but when we had passed nothing but darkened buildings, I had to wonder, "Will it be open?"

Mom and Tai-Paw both laughed. "The Celestial is open past midnight seven nights a week," Mom informed me.

All my life, I had seen Tai-Paw in my world. Now I got to see her immersed in hers—a world that I had glimpsed on brief visits with my parents.

"It's coming up right here." In her excitement, Tai-Paw tapped the glass of the window. "Get ready!"

However, the window was filled with sequin-covered T-shirts and cheap plastic toys. "They went out of business," Mom said in disappointment.

The same was true of Sarah's Cafe, which had been converted into a jewelry store. "What do people do for their desserts?" Tai-Paw sounded distressed.

As we drove farther into Chinatown, Mom and Tai-Paw were both shocked to see that one landmark after another had disappeared.

The biggest and most unpleasant surprise, though, came when we drove along Stockton. Mom pointed in horror. "Chung Jeng's is gone."

I stared at a store with heavy iron grates over the window and door. There was only empty red velvet in the window itself. "You mean that jewelry store?"

"That jewelry store used to be a comic-book place."

"Your mother used to spend hours in Chung Jeng's," Tai-Paw explained to me. "They had all sorts of comic books."

I stared at Mom. "You told me comic books were candy for the mind."

Under the pale light shed by the streetlamps, I saw Mom blush. "They are. I was trying to help you learn from my mistakes."

When we had visited Chinatown previously, it had been during the day. At night, it seemed ominously silent. As we passed one closed store after another, I shook my head. "Nothing's open. It's like they rolled up the sidewalk at six."

"No one's out walking, either," Mom said. She and Tai-Paw spoke to one another in Cantonese.

"I wish you wouldn't do that," I objected. "It makes me feel left out."

"Sorry," Mom apologized. "I was just telling Tai-Paw that a lot of things have changed."

Tai-Paw continued to stare out the window as if she were stunned. "I don't recognize anything. I could get lost in Chinatown now."

I wondered if the Thief of Hearts had felt the same way when he had reached his old home and found that time itself had stolen it. In a way, Mom and Tai-Paw sounded like thieves who had broken into their own home.

Mom swung into an alley where Hong Ch'un's cousin lived. Little light from the street slipped into the narrow alley. Tai-Paw leaned forward to look at the alcove framed in our headlights. "I know that building. I've got good friends there." She seemed relieved to find something familiar.

When Mom shut off our headlights, we were in the dark. "You didn't recognize the number?"

"Who knows numbers. I know buildings," Tai-Paw said, resting her hands on the back of the seat. "These friends both have big ears and big mouths. They'll tell us everything we need to know. Mrs. Sue loves the opera. She knows all the words. Only she can't hold a tune. Awful, awful, but you can't get her to stop. And Ah Bing was a hairdresser." She gave a little giggle. "But she has so little hair herself now that she has to wear a wig."

"Chinatown can be like a small town," Mom explained to me. "And that can be good and bad."

"And it enjoys the bad more." Tai-Paw chuckled.

"Maybe I should turn the headlights back on," Mom said to Tai-Paw. Her eyes had a hard time judging distances in dim light.

Tai-Paw looked through the window anxiously. "Maybe."

As the harsh light illuminated the alley, I slid out on my side and went to Tai-Paw's door and opened it for her.

At home, she could be quite independent, and even resentful if I was too solicitous, but that alley was a whole other world. She surprised me when she stretched out a hand. "Help me," she said.

I gave her my arm to support her while she carefully climbed out of the car. She leaned on my arm far more heavily than she did on her cane at home. I think she was a little bit afraid of falling in the dark and re-injuring herself. Step by step, we shuffled down the alley to the apartment house.

Mom was already by the door with the scrap of paper in her hand. "There are no names on the boxes, only numbers," she complained.

"Try Hong Ch'un's cousin," Tai-Paw suggested.

"Well, here goes nothing." Mom pushed the cracked, dirty white button on the box.

Through the heavy red door we heard a chime sound somewhere deep inside the apartment house. A moment later, we heard a voice coming from a distance. "What?" a woman called.

"We're looking for . . ." Mom glanced at the paper

and gave the cousin's name.

The woman answered in a rapid string of Chinese, so I looked at Mom. Mom, though, had drawn her eyebrows together. "It's a Hong Kong dialect. They speak so fast." She glanced back at us. "Tai-Paw?"

"Leave this to me." Confidently Tai-Paw patted her arm and took her place at the mailboxes. However, after pressing her ear against the door, she frowned in exasperation. "I don't recognize it either," she had to confess.

It was cool in the City though it had been hot down in Almaden. The only one dressed for the weather in Chinatown was Tai-Paw. As Mom shivered, she wrapped her arms around herself. "I didn't think I'd ever need an interpreter in Chinatown."

"I will take care of it," Tai-Paw insisted. After surveying the mailboxes, she rang a couple of bells at random before we could stop her. When we heard other voices inside, Tai-Paw called out something in loud, clear Chinese. Once again she placed her ear against the wood. Her look changed from optimistic to surprised. After a moment, she straightened up almost in a state of shock. "They've never heard of my friends."

"A lot can happen in all these years," I said.

"Yes, but I always thought I could come back. I've been away too long," Tai-Paw said sadly. "All these years, I thought it would always stay the same: my friends, the good places. But they're all gone."

I felt sorry for her. It must be hard to leave your home like Rip Van Winkle and then find everything changed when you come back. Maybe I wasn't the only one out of place and time.

"It's just a few places and a couple of people," I tried to reassure her. "The rest is the same."

Despite her many layers of clothing, Tai-Paw gave a shiver. "I don't want to know. Maybe I'd better not see any more. I want to remember Chinatown the way it was."

"What about Hong Ch'un?" Mom reminded her.

Tai-Paw squared her shoulders. "Yes. How silly of me." Setting her disappointments aside, she leaned forward again and spoke through the door. This time she nodded in relief. "There's another neighbor who's coming out, and she speaks our dialect."

It took a while before we heard dead bolts being turned, and the apartment door swung open. A small lady in a knitted brown tam-o'-shanter stared at us doubtfully.

Tai-Paw nodded and smiled and spoke quickly, showing the photo Mom had handed to her. The small lady in turn shouted back up the steps to the first occupant. The arrangement was quite clumsy and quite loud. I could see lights going on up and down the alley, as if we had woken people.

Pursing her lips, Tai-Paw translated for us. "She says that there's no one here by that name. He moved a long time ago, and she doesn't know where."

"Did Hong Ch'un come by?" Mom prompted.

Tai-Paw held another loud three-way conversation, and then spoke to us again. "Some strange girl came by, but no one could understand her because she only spoke English and Mandarin." So Hong Ch'un *was* here in Chinatown.

Mom bit her lip. "Then Hong Ch'un could be anywhere at this point."

Despite everything, I began to feel sorry for Hong Ch'un, lost somewhere in this big, dark city—a city that now seemed almost as alien to Mom and Tai-Paw as it was to me, and much more alien to Hong Ch'un.

Eight

Tai-Paw muttered, "We should see Mr. Jeh. Maybe he can help. Take me to my old place."

I was sorry Tai-Paw had gotten involved, and I was afraid that it would be yet another disappointment. "Are you sure he's still there?" I asked.

"He calls me every now and then," Tai-Paw said. "But it's been a long time." She leaned on my arm anxiously. Up to now, Tai-Paw's grip had always been light; but now I really had to support her weight.

Tai-Paw had had to shuffle before because of her bad hip; but she normally moved with a lot of energy—giving the impression that her will was much stronger than her hip.

Now, though, Tai-Paw limped slowly and heavily toward the car, as if she felt every one of her years. I suppose if I had spent so many years in one place, I would expect it to still be there when I came back.

I looked across Tai-Paw at Mom, who was supporting her on the other side. Mom, too, seemed subdued and thoughtful as we made our way back to the car.

Without a word to us, Mom pulled out and then drove around to Sacramento Street. The hill was so steep she had to slip into a lower gear. In front of us, the golden tower of the Fairmont Hotel rose high overhead as its outside elevator climbed upon a cool column of white light.

Next to the locked gates of the playground a half dozen boys lounged. They were all in their teens, with their hair swept up like plumes, and they wore expensive overcoats with the sleeves rolled back, making them look like an odd order of monks. They eyed us as we rolled past.

As Mom eased into another alley and parked, I looked around. For Tai-Paw's sake, I hoped Mr. Jeh was still alive and there. "Which was yours, Tai-Paw?" I asked her.

She pointed at a green building with iron grates over the bottom windows. "Mr. Jeh took over my room. He got tired of living with all those other old men. Now he has his own kitchen." Then she gestured toward the mirror. "I want to see."

"Just in case Mr. Jeh's in?" I teased as I tilted the rearview mirror for her.

Behind me, Tai-Paw fussed anxiously with her bandanna and pressed a finger against her lips. "Casey, do you have your lipstick?"

Despite everything, I had to laugh. "You look fine, Tai-Paw."

"Liar," Tai-Paw said.

"You really do look nice," Mom said reassuringly, but she handed over her lipstick.

When Tai-Paw had finished with her adjustments, we got out of the car and helped Tai-Paw step into the alley. While I locked up, she looked around. "They haven't painted anything," she said, scanning the walls critically.

"Hey, pretty lady, you got a cigarette?" a boy asked. Looking over my shoulder, I saw that it was the boys in the overcoats. They strolled over toward us with an insolent, feline grace.

"We don't smoke," Mom said.

One of them continued while the others drew themselves into a line across the alley.

"What you got in your purse," he demanded.

"This isn't happening," Tai-Paw murmured, as if this were all a bad dream. "Not in Chinatown."

"We'll be all right," Mom tried to reassure her, and then spoke to the boy as she pitched her purse toward him. "Just take it, okay?"

He nudged it with one pointed shoe and then jerked his head at me. "You must got something."

With my free hand, I dug out my wallet and threw it next to Mom's purse. "Here."

He leaned his head to the side lazily. "Maybe I have fun search."

For Tai-Paw this was the final indignity of the evening. Furious now, she shook free of me and Mom. "You should be ashamed of yourself. Chinese take care of one another. They don't rob each other."

He placed his right hand over his left fist and gave her a mock bow. When he straightened, though, his smile had hardened into a curving line as sharp as a knife blade. "What you got, Auntie?"

"I have nothing," Tai-Paw snapped. I had never seen her so angry—or so foolhardy. "And I am not your aunt."

"Don't talk back to them," Mom whispered to her.

However, it was as if all the disappointments of the evening had finally pushed Tai-Paw over the edge. She seemed glad to have a target for all of her fear and anger. "Why should I be afraid of this dog?" she demanded, and then launched into a Cantonese tirade that made the boy at first redden and then stiffen angrily. And behind him his friends were getting just as agitated.

All the while, Mom tried to get Tai-Paw to stop, but she wouldn't until I whispered to her, "Tai-Paw, they could hurt Mom."

Mom picked up on the idea immediately. "And Stacy."

That brought Tai-Paw back somewhat. "Here then." And contemptuously she tossed her purse at the boy.

The boy simply stepped over the purse. "Nobody call me those name."

Mom slipped in front. "Stacy, go and ring every doorbell. I'll hold him off."

I was so afraid that words wouldn't come out of my throat. All I could do was nod.

Tai-Paw, though, was still sputtering. "Chinatown is nothing but a dog pound now. Children don't make fun of old people, or rob them."

"You doan boss me around," the boy shouted. "I boss you."

At the mouth of the alley, a large man appeared with a shopping bag in his hand.

"Get out of here," the man growled.

The boy pivoted insolently, but his face lost its smile. "It's Mr. Jeh."

His friends were already retreating. He took to his heels, slipping on the slick soles of his shoes and shoving himself back up to his feet.

Mom took a couple of steps forward. "Gilbert?"

The man stood there, and then he stepped closer. "Casey? What are you doing here? I came by to check up on my great-uncle."

"You've lost some hair," Mom laughed.

"And there's more of you," he said, and shook her hand.

"Chinatown's changed," Mom said as she retrieved Tai-Paw's purse and my wallet.

"It's just a small percentage of the kids, but there are more people in Chinatown nowadays, so there are more troublemakers." Gilbert got Mom's purse and handed it to her. "You remember my dad? He was coming home late from a movie and got mugged."

"Oh, no," Mom said in alarm. "Was he hurt?"

"He broke an arm." Gilbert tapped his forearm in illustration. "So I thought that would be it. He'd just stay at home. But he likes movies so much, he still goes. If he can't do it in the daytime, he calls a cab to go the four blocks back and forth—even if it means he has to skip a meal."

"We all have to be more careful," Tai-Paw said doubtfully as she took her purse from Mom.

Gilbert stared down the alley in the direction the boys had taken. "I would have sworn I had those kids in my auto repair class."

"Them and half of Chinatown," Mom said, handing me my wallet.

I gazed at him, puzzled because the punks had called him Mr. Jeh. "This is your friend, Tai-Paw?"

Gilbert laughed. "I like to think so. But I'm also the great-nephew of her good friend." Still holding his full shopping bag, he raised his arm to indicate the apartment building.

"You used to have so much hair," Tai-Paw said by way of a greeting.

Gilbert good-naturedly ran a hand over his bald scalp. "What do you think? Should I paint it black? Or should I get Astroturf?"

"You look just fine." Mom laughed. "This is my daughter, Stacy."

I noticed that the nails of Gilbert's fingers were rimmed in black as we shook hands. "Those kids really scooted when they saw you," I said.

"They're probably scared Gilbert recognized them." Mom went up the worn red steps to the little vestibule.

"In the old days, they would have been just plain scared of me," Gilbert grumbled. "Darn punks." He seemed to take it as a personal affront that something had happened in his Chinatown.

On the left were stained, rusty mailboxes. There were plates for names, but they were left blank. On

Mom's right were doorbells. She swept her hand along the row and plunged her finger at number nine.

The door buzzed almost immediately. "Uncle is expecting me," Gilbert explained.

When Mom opened the front door, light spilled down the steps like a silken carpet. With me on one side and Gilbert on the other, Tai-Paw made her way across the alley to the sidewalk. At the base of the steps, Tai-Paw let go of Gilbert so she could take advantage of a railing. Once she had reached the doorway, Mom took her other arm.

As I followed them inside to a dim little hallway, the warmth rolled around me, along with a banquet of cooking smells. I thought I could smell frying oil, but a lot of the other scents eluded me. Even so, my stomach began to growl in answer, and I realized that I hadn't eaten since lunch.

Chinese music spilled down the steps from above, and I figured Mr. Jeh had opened his apartment door. An elderly man called something in Chinese down to us.

"Hey, Uncle," Gilbert shouted up the stairwell. "Look who I brought!"

Before Mr. Jeh could answer, Tai-Paw shouted something up to him and then tugged her bandanna forward minutely and said something to Mom in

Cantonese. Mom obligingly opened her purse and took out a compact so that Tai-Paw could fine-tune herself by the light of the apartment house.

It was slow going up the steps. Mom and Tai-Paw counted the steps as if it were a secret game between them. Gilbert and I trailed behind them, ready to brace Tai-Paw if she should falter. However, wherever there was adequate light she moved briskly. The only places she had trouble were in odd corners where the light reached only dimly. She lingered at one window, squinting. By the dim streetlight we could make out old 45's and sneakers on the roof of the building next door. "Still the same old junk." The odd landmark seemed to reassure her.

Mr. Jeh was standing in a doorway. His short hair stood up as if he had just brushed it, and he wore gray suit slacks and a knitted blue vest over a snow-white shirt. After my initial experiences with Hong Ch'un, I was a little wary of someone who was hard-core Chinese.

However, Mr. Jeh beamed at Mom and me. "It's the girl . . . and a little girl. Next time you call. You warn me. I only got these." In one hand, he held out rolls of red apricot wafers. He handed first one to me and then the other to Mom. "I know you like, you bet. And for the boy." He handed a roll of wafers to Gilbert so he wouldn't feel left out. "Now come in. All of you."

When we had all squeezed inside, he shut the door and began securing it. There were a half dozen bolts and locks on it, so it took him a little while. In the meantime, I looked around.

Mom and Tai-Paw's former home was tiny. The studio apartment couldn't have been more than ten by fifteen.

There was a narrow bed shoved lengthwise against the wall next to the doorway. Close to the wall by the door leading to the kitchen was an old record player with lots of old 78 records. Boxes were stacked neatly one on top of another next to piles of newspapers and magazines, and there was room for a small kitchen table covered by a turquoise tablecloth with red chrysanthemums.

The apartment's one window opened on a narrow light well that carried snatches of sound from the apartments above and below. Mom pivoted slowly, surveying the apartment where she had spent part of her childhood. It hardly seemed big enough for Mr. Jeh to live in, let alone Tai-Paw and Mom.

In the meantime, as Mr. Jeh helped Tai-Paw take off her coat, he said something sad to her. Upset, Tai-Paw shook her head as if his words only confirmed her bad mood, and then she said something in Chinese to Mom.

"I'm sorry," Mom said sympathetically, and then explained to me that several of their close friends had died.

Mr. Jeh was upset when he heard about what had happened outside his home. "You have to be more careful," he scolded Tai-Paw, as if it were her fault for putting "the girl and little girl" in danger.

"Chinatown's not the same," Tai-Paw complained.

"So?" Mr. Jeh asked matter-of-factly as he took her coat. "Neither are you. Neither am I, you bet. I got lot more wrinkles and lots less hair." Putting the coat on a hanger, he hung it up on a nail. "I make you some tea."

From Gilbert's sack came cartons of duck, rice, and other treats, and I was surprised at how much we wolfed down. When Gilbert heard the purpose of our errand, he set his chopsticks over his rice bowl. "Chinatown's locked up tight except for a few restaurants. If she's in the area, we should find her."

"Let's hope we get to her before those kids do," Mom said.

"You rest," Mr. Jeh insisted, and waved a hand at the roll of wafers on her lap. "You eat your dinner. Now have your candy. Leave things to me." And going to his telephone, he began to dial.

The warmth and light and company had begun to revive Tai-Paw's spirits, and she said something to Mr. Jeh. When he answered, she slapped her knee with pleasure. "He's calling up a friend of ours who washes dishes in a restaurant. He can check around the other restaurants to see if she's in one of the places that's still open."

"See?" I said to Tai-Paw. "You have plenty of friends up here."

In the meantime, Mr. Jeh had been speaking rapidly on the telephone. He looked up now from the receiver. "What does she look like?"

Mom opened her purse and dug out the photo Mrs. Wang had given her. Mr. Jeh held it in one hand at arm's distance as if he was farsighted, and as soon as he had hung up on that first friend, he began dialing again. When Tai-Paw queried him in Cantonese, he answered her.

Of all the people in the room I was the only one who didn't understand, so I tapped Mom on the knee. "What's going on?"

Gilbert, though, turned to explain. "He's going to call up another friend and have her look out her window. We'll have someone checking on every block. If she's around, we'll find her."

I thought of all those old people keeping watch like sentries upon the hills, and for the first time I began to feel confident that we would find Hong Ch'un.

"This"—Tai-Paw beamed as she pointed at Mr. Jeh—"this is the same old Chinatown."

What had Tai-Paw said about the heart's eyes? She had said something about things being okay if they were clear. I felt as if my heart's eyes had opened just at that moment, and I could look through them for the first time. So, I could see through not only my brain's eyes but also my heart's.

Nine

After a couple of dozen calls, Mr. Jeh set his phone aside and picked up the photo. "Now we go for a walk. I'll fax this to friends around the City."

It seemed a little odd to me for pensioners to have fax machines. "Are fax machines that common?"

Mr. Jeh waved his arm in a big circle. "Chinese stores all over San Francisco. Lots of them got fax."

"If you speak Cantonese," Gilbert explained, "and you want to communicate with someone who speaks Mandarin, it's easier to send a letter than to call. Whether you speak Cantonese or Mandarin, the written characters are the same."

"Will anything be open?" Tai-Paw fretted. The longer Tai-Paw and Mom talked with their friends, the stronger the lilt grew in their voices—a lilt that resembled Gilbert's and Mr. Jeh's.

"For you, always," Mr. Jeh said. "We haven't all been chased out yet."

Gilbert added, "And just because things are closed down here doesn't mean that they're closed down in other parts of the City. Anyway, most faxes are still turned on even if the places have shut down."

I was glad to see Tai-Paw perk up. Gilbert and Mr. Jeh were just the tonics she needed.

Mr. Jeh bundled up in almost as many sweaters and vests as Tai-Paw had. By the time he put on his suit coat, he had added so many inches to his trunk that he had to leave the coat open.

Since Tai-Paw had even more trouble descending than ascending, we took even more care to get her down to street level. And though Mr. Jeh moved slowly, it was almost with the same ease as Gilbert did.

It's funny, but Tai-Paw was almost as much of a tourist in Chinatown as me. As we passed by a Chinese herbal store, she stopped to peer at the strange objects floating in huge glass jars. "This place is new. And look, it's ———" And she said something in Chinese to Mr. Jeh.

He smiled with as much pride as if he had been the owner. "Now the Americans change their laws. Now you can get herbs, incense, all the right stuff."

"Finally." Tai-Paw glanced up as if trying to memorize the name of the store.

Gilbert was a step ahead of us, alertly keeping one eye on us and the other on the surroundings. "And families can get together now."

Mr. Jeh snorted. "Mine should have stayed back in China."

That surprised me. "Don't you like having your family here?"

Mr. Jeh stayed close to Tai-Paw's elbow. "All those years, I think of them. And always I think of when I see them finally, and what I say and what they say, and what I do and what they do. Everybody so happy."

Mom took a professional tack. "So the reunion didn't live up to your expectations?"

Mr. Jeh relented a little. "I guess so. Some. But my boys, they got no sense. They ask me why didn't I buy this house or that when they were cheap."

"Who had the money back then?" Tai-Paw sympathized.

Mr. Jeh jerked his head in disgust. "And I tell them they grow up in China, where everyone is Chinese. They think it always okay here. Now you live where you want and do what you like. But not back in the old days. Then you have to be very careful. Isn't that so?" Mr. Jeh appealed to Tai-Paw.

"Things change," Tai-Paw said, "and people change."

"You bet." From the gloom of his tone, Mr. Jeh

didn't sound as if he thought it was for the better.

"Keep in mind that his 'boys' are in their sixties," Gilbert whispered to me.

Mr. Jeh grunted as if it were an old argument between them. "They are boys. Buy, buy, buy—that's all they know. And their children even worse." He shuddered just thinking of them.

I thought it was funny that Mr. Jeh seemed closer to Gilbert, his great-nephew, than to his own sons. But then, Gilbert was an old Chinatowner just like Mr. Jeh.

Gilbert was inclined to be kinder toward his relations. "It's not bad to have someone in the family who knows how to make a buck."

We walked down the hill slowly, warning Tai-Paw when the pavement wasn't level or when we were nearing a set of flat iron doors that opened into a basement.

The slow pace suited the talk, since every few yards they looked at some building where one of their friends used to live or where some store had been.

I lost track after a while. I could only listen to so many names and places before I overloaded. I promised myself, though, that I'd get the information from Mom and Tai-Paw in smaller doses when we were back in Almaden.

As we passed near a playground, Tai-Paw halted so abruptly that I was caught by surprise. My forward momentum made me tug at Tai-Paw's arm so she released me.

"Your grandmother used to play basketball in a court below the clubhouse," Tai-Paw said to me.

Mom crowded excitedly beside her.

I said, "I didn't know she played."

Tai-Paw squinted through the tall cyclone fence at the elaborate jungle gym. Beyond it we saw a tall concrete building. "There used to be a clubhouse and a Ping-Pong table."

Gilbert peered over our shoulders. "They still have basketball courts inside the building."

Tai-Paw clung to the fence for a moment as if she could almost see her daughter there. "That's where your grandmother met your grandfather."

"That's kind of sweet," I said. I hadn't even known they played basketball in Chinatown back in those days.

Tai-Paw pointed toward an apartment house at the mouth of an alley lower down the hill. "Back then that house belonged to one of their friends. So when an apartment was empty, they'd all go up there and dance."

"Shameful dances," Mr. Jeh teased, and gave a little hop. Then he teased Tai-Paw. "But I see you do them too."

"You should see the dances now." Tai-Paw put a hand to her mouth. "Oh, what was his name?"

"It was my uncle Sherman who owned the building," Gilbert said. "He sold it to a Hong Kong group ten years ago. Triple the rent now."

While they began to talk real estate, I looked up at the apartment house. One of the windows was lit, and against the window shade I could almost imagine seeing the silhouettes of my grandparents hopping or whirling or however they danced back then.

I turned to ask Tai-Paw if she remembered, but they were still busy talking about the rents of various apartments and stores. So I made yet another mental note to ask Tai-Paw some other time.

For Tai-Paw and Mr. Jeh and Mom and Gilbert, every building in Chinatown contained some memories, so when they talked about rents and prices, it was a chance to revisit a world that was gone and relive moments in the past.

"And the new Hong Kong landlords want three thousand a month," Mr. Jeh was saying. "*Three thousand.* Do you know how much chow mein you got to sell?"

Mom rolled her eyes upward as she calculated. "Something like six thousand orders?"

Mr. Jeh waved a hand in disgust. "So the restaurant

just stands empty. Stupid to be so greedy."

As Tai-Paw turned away from the playground, she held out her arm and I took it. "Before the ———— was a restaurant"—I didn't catch the Chinese name—"it used to be a nightclub. When your grandparents graduated from high school, they and their classmates rented the club. And then they all dressed up. Oh, they looked so handsome and so pretty," she added with a sigh, "but all that's gone now."

"You bet," Mr. Jeh agreed.

I glanced at Mom, who was strolling on the other side of Tai-Paw. I had heard more about my grandparents in Chinatown than about her. "So what was it like when you were here, Mom?"

"I was very good," Mom said angelically.

Gilbert laughed at that, and even Mr. Jeh and Tai-Paw had to smile. "With a left cross and a hook." Gilbert shadowboxed. "No one messed with your mother, Stacy."

I stared in amazement at Mom. "This from the woman who never let me look at 'Tom and Jerry' cartoons because they were too violent?"

Mom shot an annoyed look at Gilbert. I think that if I hadn't been there, she might have unleashed her left cross and hook on Gilbert for revealing the deep, dark secrets of her past. "Some of us grow up, Stacy, and realize there are other ways to settle disputes."

"Too many kids pack guns nowadays," Gilbert agreed. "You were smart not to fight those punks who tried to mug you. Me, I haven't got brains like you."

"What do you mean? You're a teacher too," Mom insisted.

Gilbert shrugged, but he was pleased that Mom thought he was smart.

I took the opportunity to point at the storefronts with curtains hung in front of the windows. "What's in those places?"

"Sweatshops," Mom explained. "Inside, women assemble American clothes from pieces. Shirts, blouses, dresses. Some of them get sold in the fanciest stores."

"A lot of the sweatshops have moved out of Chinatown too," Gilbert said.

"They'll be just as stifling wherever they are," Mom observed. "Because they'll be owned by the same people." She pointed at one concealed by curtains with blue and yellow polka dots. "Does Pinky still own that?"

"Naw," Gilbert said. "He sold out a long time ago. His kid is a big-time fashion designer back in New York."

"Why'd they call him Pinky?" I asked Mom.

"Well"—Mom tried to fight back a smile and failed—"he was famous for playing tricks on new people he hired. I'd gotten a job cleaning up and doing other odd jobs."

I thought about the tiny studio apartment she had once shared with Tai-Paw. I already knew that her mother had died when she was young, but I hadn't known her father had gambled. Her childhood couldn't have been much fun. I'd had it easy compared to her—which was perhaps why she was impatient sometimes.

"After your paper route?" I asked.

She nodded her head and went on. "Now, when you cut the pieces from the fabric, you used a special kind of saw on a pile of fabric so you could cut a lot of pieces at the same time. I hadn't been there more than an hour when he screamed and held up his hand." She held up her own hand to show four fingers. "And he said that he had cut off his little finger and asked me to find it. So I got down on my hands and knees and went looking, and I found something that looked like a little finger. And then he had me get a big jar of glue and try to put it back on. Only when I tried to, he had five fingers again." She put up her little finger in illustration. "What I had thought was a little finger was an American sausage. He'd even warmed it up so it'd fool me. Pinky was good."

As Mom laughed at the memory, she seemed to shed years. It was a part of Mom that I had never seen before, even on our brief excursion up to the City. She really did belong to the old Chinatown—just as Tai-Paw did. The middle-aged professional, Dr. Casey Young Palmer, who could skewer you with a sideways glance and the right question—that was the only side of her I'd known up until now.

I couldn't get over what she had told me. "So you held down a job besides a paper route."

She squeezed Tai-Paw's arm affectionately. "Your Tai-Paw had me saving for college even then."

Tai-Paw looked at Mom with a love and confidence so fierce that I don't think Mom would've had any choice even if she hadn't wanted to. "Sewing is for people like me," Tai-Paw declared. "Not for you."

I hadn't known how difficult it had been for Mom to get where she was. I began to understand why Mom drove herself so hard, and why she tried to make me do the same. I'd try to remember this the next time we got into one of our "discussions" about my own attitude. I just wished that someone believed in me as fiercely as Tai-Paw did in Mom. I wished Mom did.

"What other jobs did you do?" I wondered.

"Whatever would pay an honest buck." Mom's shoulders hunched defensively. "You don't really want to hear. You'd just get bored."

I almost thought I could see the young girl who had walked these same streets with Tai-Paw. "Even with Tai-Paw's help, it couldn't have been easy."

I could only guess at the kind of drive that had taken her to college and beyond. "Tell me more," I urged.

She drew her eyebrows together in puzzlement. "You always complain so much when I get together with my Chinatown friends down in Almaden. What is it you call it?" She hunted for the phrase and then enunciated it carefully, "My 'Chinese love fests.'"

I could feel my cheeks reddening because she must have overheard one of my mutterings. "I never knew the places before." I glanced around the street. "But after tonight I feel like I know a little bit more."

She considered it while she surveyed the street herself. "I keep forgetting that you and your father can't see things with my eyes. There was a time when I felt like a real outsider here too."

"You too?" I asked in surprise.

"I didn't come to live here until I was about your age," she explained.

Normally I would have avoided saying too much that would leave me open for another one of her critiques, but I couldn't help telling her, "I like it when you talk about yourself and Tai-Paw. It's interesting. But a lot of other times I don't know who or what you're talking about."

Mom pursed her lips in a little smile. "I should have seen the distinction."

"You can't know everything, Mom," I said, and then had to concede, "I don't think I understood the difference myself."

Mom fiddled with her bracelet. "I thought it was me who was boring."

"Not after I've borrowed your eyes for a while," I admitted.

"So your old mom isn't a nerd?" she asked almost shyly.

"Just your slang," I said. "But nothing else."

"I used to dress in sweatshirts and jeans," she confessed.

"You did? But now your clothes and jewelry are always in good taste," I assured her. "There isn't a mother who could top you."

"Sometimes," she confessed, "I feel like everybody's going to find out I'm just an impostor, and they'll ship me back to Chinatown."

"And you think I'm going to rat on you?" I asked.

She leaned her head to the side as she considered that. "Maybe it's easier to point out your faults before you can point out mine."

I felt choked up. "And I thought you didn't approve of me."

She smiled, embarrassed. "Funny, I thought the same about you."

We were both a little afraid to be the first one, but finally Mom raised an arm. I went and let her hug me.

Over her shoulder, I saw Mr. Jeh peering at something. "So you still have it." He pointed at her wrist.

As I stepped away, Mom held out the charm on the bracelet. "I wouldn't be without it."

Between them seemed to be some unspoken secret. In a way, it made me feel sad to discover that there was a lot more to Mom than her prosperous life in the suburbs. However, even if she had a community up here as well as one down in Almaden, I still didn't. I felt like a double outcast now.

At the mouth of the alley, Gilbert had paused to scan the darkened doorways for trouble.

Ahead I saw that the store doors and windows were protected by heavy iron bars. "Is it safe?" I asked, remembering the punks. "Maybe we shouldn't walk too far at night."

Gilbert turned to me. "Don't judge Chinatown by what just happened. You've got to keep your eyes open here all the time, but that's true of any place in the City nowadays.

"It's not really a rough street. Those stores have bars because they sell jewelry," he explained.

As we passed by, though, there was only empty red

velvet in each window, the jewels and gold all having been stored away.

"You got to buzz-buzz. Then they open if they think you're rich." Mr. Jeh pantomimed jabbing a door button with his thumb.

"Everything's turning into a fortress, though," Gilbert said. "Even Casey's old school, St. Mary's, is locked up tight in the daytime."

"But you work here," I said, keeping one eye out for Hong Ch'un.

"Maybe I'm stubborn." Gilbert grinned at me sideways. "Or maybe I'm just stupid."

"No," Mr. Jeh insisted. "This is home." He beckoned to me. "You come in the daytime. It's all different then. People everywhere, to school or to work or shop for food. Come up again and visit me. Bring your great-grandmom."

"It'd take forever then." Mom linked arms with Tai-Paw. "You couldn't walk more than twenty feet without bumping into someone who knew your Tai-Paw." She swung her arm in a broad, choppy arc. "So then you'd finish and try to go on and after twenty feet you'd meet someone else. It could take a couple of hours just to buy a pound of oranges."

Tai-Paw patted Mom on the arm. "Don't make up stories."

Gilbert leaned forward with a laugh. "It's true,

Auntie. Twenty feet and talk, twenty feet and talk."

"Those days are gone," Tai-Paw said. "So many of our friends are dead, or gone."

"What do you mean? There's still plenty," Mr. Jeh insisted.

Gilbert nodded to Mr. Jeh. "When I walk with Uncle, it's just like that."

"What would they think of me?" I asked cautiously.

Mr. Jeh didn't hesitate. "That you're very pretty. And if they say anything else, you tell them to come up and I'll talk to them, you bet." Something about the gleam in his eye suggested that he would do more than talk.

And it made me feel good inside to belong to something, even if it was only the group walking along the narrow sidewalk. What had Tai-Paw said when she told me about the Thief of Hearts? When one world ends, you find another. Just like Mom had. Maybe you even make your own.

Ten

$\mathbf{M}$r. Jeh led us to some kind of wedding shop. The banner declared that the designer was famous throughout Hong Kong. The orange-and-white tuxes were bad enough, but the wedding dresses were even worse. There was one that was all flounces edged with silver sequins. The poor mannequin looked as if she were drowning in metallic foam. And even a Las Vegas floor show wouldn't have touched some of the other, flashier wedding outfits.

"My grandson marry a Hong Kong girl. This is her shop. She let me sweep up here for five bucks," he explained, fishing in his pocket for a ring of keys. "I can't understand her Chinese, so we talk to one another in English." Holding the jingling ring at arm's length up toward the streetlight, he selected a key and opened the door.

"Come in, come in." He waved us inside with a friendly twist of his wrist.

We entered single file into the darkened store past the mannequins. In their costumes, they looked like inverted flowers. When we were all inside, he locked the door again and then sidled around us all.

"This way," he said.

In the dark, Tai-Paw clung to my arm as I followed Mr. Jeh into an office at the back of the store.

When he flicked on a switch, we could see that the office was crammed full of boxes and filing cabinets. Mr. Jeh hunted around amid the stacks of paper upon the desk for the fax machine. "Gilbert," he said, "there's a chair there." He pointed at a pile of boxes.

Dubiously Gilbert began to lift the boxes to the side, and sure enough uncovered a chair. With a sigh, Tai-Paw settled on the chair to wait.

She and Mom made chitchat with Gilbert while Mr. Jeh wrote out something on a sheet of paper. Then, attaching the photo with tape, he set it in the fax machine. Punching in the number, he tried to send it through, but the photo stuck in the machine.

Grumbling, he had to get Gilbert to help him move some other boxes aside to reveal a small copy machine. When he had copied the photo, he handed it back to Mom and then tried to fax the letter and photocopied picture.

He gave the fax machine a pleased pat when it accepted the two sheets. He did it about a dozen more times before he folded up the sheets and put them into his pocket. "There. These friends will fax other friends. We'll have the whole city looking for her now."

He waited until we had filed out before he turned off the light. Then he moved in front of us to open the door. When we were all outside, he locked up again.

"We'll find her, you bet," he promised.

After we returned to Mr. Jeh's place, we warmed up some tea. We had just finished our third cup when we got a call from one of Tai-Paw and Mr. Jeh's friends. Hong Ch'un had been spotted sitting in a doorway.

Since we needed to get there fast, we decided to take the car. Tai-Paw insisted on coming along, so naturally Mr. Jeh said he would accompany us. Gilbert also came along, saying that he wanted to know the outcome of the story. The car was pretty cramped as we wound our way through Chinatown.

As Mom swung us down a street toward Grant Avenue, she glanced at the window displays of the surrounding souvenir stores. "Well, these seem a lot more Chinese than when I was a kid."

However, as we drove along, there seemed to be a lot less of them. Instead, the stores sold cameras or fancy statues like Lladro. Mr. Jeh nodded to them. "They're not even run by Chinese."

"And they're the kind of stores you could find any

place you've got tourists," Gilbert added. "Fisherman's Wharf or downtown or Disneyland."

"I never thought the souvenir stores were the heart of Chinatown anyway," Mom argued.

"What is?" I wondered.

"We are," Tai-Paw said quietly.

And I found myself wishing that I could feel a connection as deeply as they did.

As we passed under the various neon signs, rainbows seemed to flicker across Mr. Jeh's face as he nudged Tai-Paw accusingly. "See. That's why you should come back. How can you live down there?"

"There are plenty of Chinese down there, too," Tai-Paw said. "I can buy anything I want down there. And the restaurants down there are just as good as the ones up here." They would have been a lively couple at any age.

"That's not what you say when I bring things home," Mom said.

"I don't want you to get smug," Tai-Paw said as she pulled her bandanna from her pocket. We had been in such a rush that she had not been able to put it on until now.

"You miss Chinatown and Chinatown misses you. Come back," Mr. Jeh urged.

For a moment, I thought Tai-Paw might give in. I

found myself wanting to beg her to stay because I had come to realize just how special she was to me. If she left, she would leave such a big hole in my life. But I also knew that I couldn't be selfish, so instead I found myself holding my breath so tight that my chest ached.

To my relief, though, she shook her head. "No, I like the birds and the trees and the flowers. Stacy's father is a very good gardener. We'll bring you some of his cherries. It's all very pretty down there. It reminds me of my village back in China—but without all the stinks."

The rheumatism in her shoulder must have been bothering her, because she was having trouble draping the bandanna over her head. I did it for her. "Stinks?" I asked.

"Where you have farms," Mom explained, "you have manure."

Mr. Jeh patted first Tai-Paw's shoulder and then Mom's. "You got Chinatown inside, you bet."

Tai-Paw leaned toward me so I could tie the bandanna under her chin. "If it's in me, then it doesn't matter where the rest of me lives," she argued. Her voice had a warning edge, as if she was daring him to contradict her. "I crossed a big ocean to come here. Why can't I go a few more miles to the south?"

I wondered if Tai-Paw had acted like Hong Ch'un

did when she first came to America. I decided that she hadn't. Tai-Paw was too openminded and too eager to learn new things to make Hong Ch'un's mistakes.

"You could come to visit us," Mom offered to Mr. Jeh. "I'll even pick you up."

"I'm too old for birds and flowers." Mr. Jeh grunted in disappointment.

Gilbert leaned forward in anticipation, peering through the windshield intently. "Slow down. There." He pointed to a white shape in a doorway.

As Mom stopped the car, a man in a dazzling white shirt stepped out onto the sidewalk, waving his arm. While Gilbert rolled down the front window, the man squeezed between two parked cars and into the street. Nodding hello to Mr. Jeh in the back, he seemed surprised and delighted to see Tai-Paw. However, for the moment, he was concentrating on the business at hand.

"I hear dis noise from de store's garbage can," he said quietly. "So I d'ink it's cats again. Only it's dat girl. She's around de corner."

I really felt sorry for Hong Ch'un then, scrounging for food in a garbage can. If you lived like a princess, it must be pretty hard to fall that far and that fast. I lost any taste I had for revenge.

As we got out of the car, though, Tai-Paw insisted on coming along too. "It's pretty dark," I warned her.

"You help me," she said, clutching at my arm. As we maneuvered toward the parked cars, I saw that the man's store sold Chinese books and magazines.

"You shouldn't have let her eat from a garbage can," Mr. Jeh scolded the man.

"She's not eating. She's reading," the man said indignantly.

"Of course," Tai-Paw whispered as we helped her shuffle between the parked cars. "Her father said she had enough money to get up here, but not for much else. Where would you go to escape, then?"

"You mean like from prison?" I asked.

"No, in your mind," Tai-Paw said. With one firm, decisive step, she mounted the sidewalk.

"I give up," Mom said from behind. We were like two tugboats guiding an ocean liner into the docks.

Tai-Paw looked over her shoulder at Mom. "Think about where you always went."

"I read American comic books," Mom said after a moment.

Tai-Paw nodded her head triumphantly. "And she would want to find Chinese ones."

"I got all kinds," the storekeeper boasted. "Most of them from Hong Kong."

Sure enough, Hong Ch'un was sitting on her legs in a doorway, body tilted toward the streetlamp as she turned the pages of a black-and-white comic. Next to her feet was a stack of more discarded comic books.

"Hong Ch'un," Mom said softly.

Her head shot up, but when she saw me, she darted from the doorway. Gilbert made a grab for her, but he missed and went falling onto the sidewalk.

I left Tai-Paw to Mom and took off after her, but Hong Ch'un was fast.

"Hong Ch'un, wait!" I panted.

Puffing, Hong Ch'un hesitated. The black-and-white Chinese comic was in her hand. From the pages I had seen in the light of the streetlamp, it looked like a romance comic. "What do you want?" she asked suspiciously.

I made myself stand still. I didn't want any quick moves to startle her into running again. "We've come to take you home. Your parents are frantic."

Hong Ch'un swung her eyes toward me in open challenge. "Do you think I'm the thief?"

I hesitated, still unsure. But I knew it wasn't me, so it had to be her. As far as I was concerned, it was payback time. "After calling me what you did, how can you expect me to side with you?"

She pressed her lips together into a thin line. "You remember too well."

"I have a good memory for wrongs," I said softly.

"That makes you Chinese." She smiled ruefully. "I said something I shouldn't have." And she bowed her head to me. "I'm sorry if I ever offended you. So many things are strange and different here. I was scared and angry, and I made you the target, but I did not take those things."

The apology seemed so heartfelt that my convictions began to waver a little more. She didn't seem capable of being so mean. If Hong Ch'un wasn't the real Thief of Hearts, who was? There had been no secret about the value of each object to the owner. And plenty of people had had the opportunity to steal them. It could even have been Jeff, the perpetual practical joker, who had pretended to lose his own treasure to throw off suspicion. And yet how had the things gotten into the backpack in my locker?

Tai-Paw, though, could see with the heart's eyes. "Of course you're not the thief," she said from behind me.

"I tried to tell them." The comic book dropped from Hong Ch'un's hand, and she ran right by me to Tai-Paw, who let go of Mom so she could hold out both arms.

Hong Ch'un went right into them and gave Tai-Paw a big hug, and she continued to hold her as she began to cry. I almost felt jealous as I first picked up the comic book she had dropped and then got the others.

Eleven

Hong Ch'un had replaced me as one of Tai-Paw's supporters as we returned to the car. Despite all of her professional training, Mom resorted to a simple, reassuring pat on the back. "Everything will be all right."

"How?" Hong Ch'un demanded through her tears. "Everyone still thinks I'm guilty. But someone else took those things."

That was too much. First she had taken Tai-Paw and now she was trying to take my reputation. "Don't try to shift the blame to me," I snapped.

"Why would she do a thing like that?" Mom asked.

"I was the only other person who had access to her backpack, because it was in *my* locker," I explained.

Tai-Paw halted before she looked back at me. "But I know you're no thief either, so it must be someone else."

"How?" I asked her.

"I know you," she nodded to me and then to Hong

Ch'un, "and I know Hong Ch'un."

Personally I thought half of Tai-Paw's faith was misplaced, so I didn't say anything, but Hong Ch'un agreed with her eagerly. "Then your word is enough for me," she said. "It isn't either of us."

Tai-Paw shuffled toward her. "Hong Ch'un, how much do you want to prove you're innocent?"

"More than anything," Hong Ch'un said.

"Then," Tai-Paw said, picking up the pace once she was on solid concrete, "you have to set a trap."

"You've been watching too many detective shows." Mom laughed. "But it would be nice if it worked." It was plain that Mom didn't give Tai-Paw's idea much chance of success because she put on her level, professional voice. "But if you want, Hong Ch'un, you can come over tomorrow evening so we can talk."

Hong Ch'un mumbled a thank you and did not speak again until we reached the car. Gilbert and Mr. Jeh decided to walk back to Mr. Jeh's place, so Mom lingered to thank them, along with the storekeeper—as well as to return the comic books.

In the meantime, as Hong Ch'un and I helped Tai-Paw get into the car, Tai-Paw glanced at Mom to make sure she was busy and then whispered to Hong Ch'un. "To set the trap, we'd need to make the real thief think it's safe to steal again. So you'd have to go back to school. People will stare and talk. Can you be strong enough?"

"I'll try anything. I have to prove I'm innocent," Hong Ch'un said so earnestly that I began to believe she wasn't acting.

Tai-Paw plopped down on the rear seat. "I thought so, but you'll need help to bait the trap."

I didn't relish the idea of going back to school any more than Hong Ch'un did, but Hong Ch'un turned to me in her desperation. "Please help me, Stacy."

Still, I hesitated.

"Shh, here comes Casey," Tai-Paw warned as she buckled her seatbelt. "We'll talk about this later when she's not around. She's very smart, but she trusts people too much. She thinks they will always do the right thing if you just ask them. She wouldn't approve of traps."

Mom opened the car door on the driver's side. In her hands she held the pile of discarded comic books. "The storekeeper said you can keep them, Hong Ch'un."

While she slid behind the wheel, she handed them to me to pass along to Hong Ch'un. When I turned in the front seat, I saw that Tai-Paw was holding Hong Ch'un's hand to reassure her. I fought back another momentary twinge of jealousy as Tai-Paw held out her hand and gave my arm an affectionate squeeze.

As we drove toward the freeway, Mom said to Tai-Paw, "I'll try to find the Chinese station." Keeping one hand on the wheel, she fiddled with the radio. As she did, her owl charm clicked against the plastic of the steering wheel.

It drew the attention of Hong Ch'un, who seemed eager to find some point in common now. "That looks Chinese."

"My grandmother asked her friend Mr. Jeh to make it for me." Mom held it up so they could see the streaked sides of the carving.

"What's the stone?" Hong Ch'un asked, curious.

"It's ————," Tai-Paw said in Cantonese, which left Hong Ch'un as puzzled as ever so Tai-Paw reached over and tapped the back of Mom's seat. "What's the word?"

"'Dream stone,'" Mom translated. "You see it used for seals." She mimed using a seal on a letter.

Hong Ch'un leaned between the two seats to examine it closer. "But what is the animal?"

"It's an owl," Mom explained.

Hong Ch'un scratched her head in puzzlement. "But there's nothing lucky about owls. They're evil, disrespectful animals. Why would you want one?"

Mom wriggled her wrist a little so that the owl

danced. "Maybe in China, but in America owls are wise."

As Hong Ch'un settled back, she made it clear whose mythology she trusted. "I still wouldn't wear one," she said disapprovingly.

As Chinese poured from the radio, Mom restored her other hand to the wheel. "Do you think your parents would have wanted you to run away from school?"

"No," Hong Ch'un said.

"So, in a way, it was disrespectful to them," Mom suggested.

"Yes," Hong Ch'un admitted reluctantly.

"And yet," Mom coaxed, "it was smart to get away from your tormentors."

"So you can be both smart and disrespectful for the same thing," Hong Ch'un said thoughtfully.

"You'll find that happening a lot as you learn to adjust," Mom said. "If you need someone to talk to, you can always call me. Honest, I'd like to help."

"Thank you," Hong Ch'un said cautiously. "You're a very smart woman. How do you help people? Do you report them?"

Mom nodded. "If it's necessary."

Hong Ch'un sighed as if she understood. "And then they receive correction?"

There was something about the word that gave me

the chills, and Mom squirmed in her seat. "Correction?" she asked. "Just what kind of wrongs did you have in mind?"

"Anything that harms society." Hong Ch'un almost sounded as if she were parroting a phrase from a book.

Mom stopped for a red light. "I'd report physical harm, but were you referring to politics, as well?"

Hong Ch'un seemed really on her guard now. "Everything seems to concern you."

Mom put the car into neutral. "I'm a psychologist; I'm not a government spy. Here you can have any opinion you want on politics."

Hong Ch'un only trusted Tai-Paw. "Really?" she asked her.

"You can talk and talk and talk," Tai-Paw assured her. "It won't matter."

"My parents are so careful when they talk." Hong Ch'un sounded relieved. "They grew up at a time when you had to be. When my father graduated from college, he spent five years on a pig farm feeding pigs."

Curiosity got the better of me, so I turned around in the front seat. "What has talking got to do with that? I have a cousin who went up to Oregon to become a weaver after he got his degree in chemistry from Berkeley. He just wanted to get back to nature."

Hong Ch'un smiled with one corner of her mouth. "My father was being re-educated. The Red Guard said he was too elitist and needed tempering."

Maybe I should have watched some of those PBS specials with Mom, but of course, I had avoided them like the plague. "What's the Red Guard?" I wondered.

Hong Ch'un paused the way someone does before trying to explain a complicated subject. "The Red Guard were young people who thought they were going to restore the purity of the Revolution. They would go into people's houses and lecture them. They made all sorts of people march through the street wearing dunce caps."

I understood a little about why she had been so aloof this morning. I suppose if I came from a place like that, I would also be wary of strangers. "But you said you lived in a big house with a garden," I said, "so somebody must have tried to make up for what happened."

She pantomimed hanging up clothes. "We lived in a big house, but we shared it with a dozen other families. The orchard had gotten chopped down for firewood, and the garden had gone to weeds. We hung out our laundry there." She smiled. "But I made you think it was our estate."

So she had a sense of humor after all. "Your jokes

are a lot like Sylvia's," I said as Mom stopped for a red light.

Holding the clasp of her own seat belt, she studied Tai-Paw's to see how it was done. "Sylvia?"

I remembered my own seat belt then. "The girl with the rabbit's foot."

Hong Ch'un jammed the clasp into the buckle angrily. "I am not at all like her. She has a wicked heart."

As I clicked my own clasp and buckle together, I defended Sylvia. "The kids at school aren't the Red Guard."

"All of that happened before I was born," she said, testing the belt. "But when they went into my backpack, I remembered my parents' stories."

I suppose I would have run away this afternoon too if my father had gone through that. "You said parents. Did something happen to your mother, too?" I thought of that nervous woman who had appeared on our doorstep.

Hong Ch'un folded her hands. "My mother was a poet," Hong Ch'un said, "but the Red Guard made her burn all her own books because they were contaminated with decadent bourgeois thought. And after that, she was afraid to write down any poems. If they had found them, they might have really punished her."

Mom put on her own seat belt. "She gave up writing poems?"

"Oh, no," Hong Ch'un said. "She still made them, but in her head so that they could find nothing. Only they got her anyway. She wound up digging turnips. But while she dug she repeated her poems to herself over and over. Later, when the Red Guard were disbanded, she came home and wrote all of them down."

When the light changed, Mom put the car into drive again and started forward. "Maybe I can help get them translated," she offered.

Hong Ch'un turned to stare out the window. "She left them all back in China because they were painful reminders of what happened. After she wrote down the last poem, she did not write another. She had all the poems stored away, and when she let them all out in a flood, she said she was dried up inside."

"How sad," I said. "Do you remember any of them?"

When Hong Ch'un looked away from the window, I saw that her breath had left a patch on the glass. "No, unfortunately, but I recall a little bit of her favorite. The . . . the . . . what do you call professors who dig in the dirt for buried cities?"

"Archaeologists?" I suggested.

"Archaeologists," she repeated the word as if savoring the syllables; and then she said, "The archaeologists, they found an ancient tomb that's two thousand years old. Inside was a woman in a suit all of jade. My mother wrote about her. My mother said she was sleeping inside a suit so beautiful and yet cold, and within the suit she dreamed wonderful things as she waited to wake up."

"Like your mother," I sighed.

Hong Ch'un echoed my words. "It is sad." For once, we agreed on something.

"What will you tell your parents about today?" I wondered.

Hong Ch'un spoke with a kind of dignity. "I will tell my father the truth, and then we will tell my mother as much as we dare."

"She wouldn't take it well?" Mom asked.

"Many things make her . . . nervous," Hong Ch'un said matter-of-factly.

My heart went out to her right then. She seemed to accept as a natural fact that she had to protect her mother. "It must be very lonely for you," I said.

She had Tai-Paw's toughness. "I'm used to it."

There had been times today when I had felt alone and apart, especially in Chinatown. Maybe we weren't so far apart after all.

In fact, let's suppose I could look more Chinese for a while. What would happen if I went to China? I would probably make as many mistakes as Hong Ch'un had made here. Maybe even more. I began to think that

Tai-Paw was right and that I should have given her the benefit of the doubt.

"I said some things as well today," I admitted. "I'm sorry."

"No, the fault was mine," she insisted.

I had seen a Sherlock Holmes movie once. He said that if you can rule out all the possibilities, you have to accept the impossible. So, if she really wasn't the thief, I should assume that the Thief of Hearts had gotten into my locker somehow and planted the stuff in Hong Ch'un's backpack.

We might have to wait forever for someone to uncover the real identity of the thief. No, somebody was going to have to prove Hong Ch'un innocent, and it was going to have to be us. However, I had to be careful what I said so Mom wouldn't understand. Tai-Paw was right. She wouldn't approve of tricking anybody, even a thief.

"About that favor you asked for, Tai-Paw," I said, "I'll do it."

"Good girl," Tai-Paw grunted her approval. She stole a surreptitious look at Mom, but she was occupied with traffic. Feeling safe, she touched Hong Ch'un's knee. "You'll be at school tomorrow?"

"Of course," Hong Ch'un said. When I saw how hopeful she looked, it made me believe that I had made the right decision. "You've been so kind. Can I help with the favor?"

"No, just show up tomorrow," Tai-Paw told her.

"I will," Hong Ch'un promised eagerly.

As we swung onto the freeway, I tried to think of other suspects for the Thief of Hearts, but after a while my head started to hurt. We'd just have to go ahead and do it.

Twelve

At Tai-Paw's own request, Mom dropped off Tai-Paw and me first.

"Perhaps I should call my parents," Hong Ch'un suggested timidly.

"I gave Gilbert the number to tell them you were safe," Mom said, and looked over her shoulder for a second. "Don't worry. I'll go in with you."

Hong Ch'un smiled nervously. "Thank you."

Our house lay in the moonlight like some sleepy beast, and I was looking forward to bed when I saw a familiar shape upon the roof silhouetted against the bright full moon.

"Oh, dear," Mom said when she recognized Dad. "The wind must finally be right."

Tai-Paw murmured as the car pulled up on the driveway alongside Dad's, "I didn't realize it was that time of year so soon."

Mom killed the engine and cut the lights. "Don't anyone get out. I don't want to startle your father."

Still in a suit and tie, Dad struggled up the slanting shingles holding a severed branch in front of him.

Hong Ch'un's head appeared between the two front seats. "What is he doing?" she asked, totally mystified.

"My husband is pollinating his cherry tree," Mom explained. "When we first moved down here, we didn't have to worry about pollinating our trees because the winds swept in pollen from the orchards. But now all the orchards have been torn up so that houses could be built."

I always thought it was weird that there are boy cherry trees and girl cherry trees. I can't tell the difference, but my dad can. So every season he found a branch to pollinate his.

Hong Ch'un was still bewildered. "But why doesn't he just hold his branch over your tree?"

"He feels it's his civic duty," I explained. "You never know if there might be some lone surviving cherry tree hidden away in someone else's backyard."

"He's a good person," Hong Ch'un said with fervent approval.

Dad had finally managed to ascend to the top of the roof. The moonlight made his white shirt glow with a magical light as he stood with a foot perched on either slanting side.

Silent spectators inside the car, we watched my father raise the tree branch overhead. Dad was slightly bald, so when the breeze ruffled his hair it rose like the points of a golden crown. He held the branch in front of him intently until the breeze picked up, whipping pollen and petals from the branch and sending them darting around like little pastel gnats. In the moonlight, the petals looked like pixie dust.

Solemn as a priest, my father shook the branch first to the left, then to the right, then to the front of him, repeating his movements with ritual precision. As he waved the branch, pollen and petals rose up in a silvery, hazy cloud, softening his outline as it rose into the night sky toward the moon.

"He looks so graceful," Hong Ch'un said in a low voice. "It's almost like a dance."

Turning slowly, the branch trailing streamers of pollen around him, Dad shook his branch toward the last of the four directions, completing his benediction over the rest of the neighborhood.

"Your cherries must be wonderful," Hong Ch'un said.

"The birds get most of them," I said, sighing, "but Dad promises cherries to so many people that we usually wind up buying them from the supermarket."

On the roof, Dad threw away the branch with a forward push of his arms. The branch, still trailing thin ribbons of pollen, fell through the air to crash down on the backyard patio.

As he began a slow, cautious descent, Mom laughed with relief. "Sometimes I think my husband loves his cherry tree more than he does us or he'd never risk breaking his neck at night."

When Dad had safely reached the ladder at the side of the house, Mom turned on the engine again. "Tell your father we're going to have a little talk when I get back."

"I don't think it will work," I warned as I got out. I helped Tai-Paw from the car and stood with her as Mom turned on her headlights and backed down the driveway.

With one final wave to Hong Ch'un, Tai-Paw held on to my arm. "Let's hurry. I have to talk to your father."

In the meantime, though, Dad had already scooted back into the house. "Welcome!" he boomed from the front door.

As he stepped onto the porch, the smell of hot, fresh popcorn followed him outside. "I figured out your ETA pretty good, so I nuked some popcorn."

"How did you know?" I asked. The odor of fresh popcorn almost made me drool.

"Your mom asked Gilbert to call me," Dad said. "Shall I whip up some mugs of hot chocolate, too?"

He was a great dad. "I'd love it," I said, helping myself to a handful of popcorn. "By the way, Mom's ticked off about your climbing the roof at night."

"She'll get over it," Dad said amiably. He was easygoing about most things, but there was a stubborn core.

By the time we finished telling Dad everything that had happened, he had made some mugs of instant chocolate. Then, helping herself to a single kernel of popcorn at a time, Tai-Paw mentioned her idea.

Dad was a lot better sport about things than Mom was; but then, he liked all sorts of games—and this was a new one. "You just need the right bait," Dad said as he delivered the steaming mugs to the table.

Tai-Paw patted his arm approvingly. "I knew you'd agree. I've got just the thing." Rising, she shuffled off to her room.

I thought about what I had just seen Mom and Tai-Paw go through in Chinatown. "Is there a place that you miss, Dad?" I asked him.

"Naw." He yawned. Dad could talk your ear off about his three passions: football, cooking, and good nutrition. However, when he strayed beyond those subjects, he resorted to answers of only one syllable.

Tonight, though, I wasn't going to let him get away with it, so I nudged him. "I'm serious."

Dad seemed so reluctant, you might have thought I'd asked him to walk across burning coals. "You're getting to be more like your mother every day."

I wasn't sure if that was a compliment, but I treated it like one anyway. "Flattery will get you nowhere."

Dad set his mug down and rubbed the spot where I had poked him. "What's gotten into you? You hate it when I talk about being a kid."

"That's because all you do is talk about the 49ers." I clinked my nail against the side of his ceramic mug. "I want to know important stuff."

Dad shrugged. "When your dad's in the Army, you move around a lot, so you never really have a home." He studied the steam rising from the surface of the chocolate before he spoke again. "But if there was one place that came close, it was San Francisco. I guess that's why I came back here to go to school," he added. "And met your mom. And then created our own junior interrogator."

"But you never seem to want to visit the City," I said.

He scratched his stomach. "I got my memories of the Presidio when my dad was in the Army. Home is here. It's funny about when I was a kid. I always wanted a place where I could grow things. Other kids wanted to fly fighters or drive tanks, but I wanted to be a farmer. You know, grow something with these two paws," he said, holding up his hands. "And then I'd eat it."

I thought of all the trouble that Dad went through for his dumb old tree. "So the cherry tree makes it home."

"Yeah, I guess." He grinned sheepishly. "Kind of stupid, isn't it?"

"No." In fact, I wondered if I could glue the stems of some ripe cherries to the tree so Dad would think he had a bumper crop. Maybe I could get Karen to help.

"Here we are." Shuffling back in, Tai-Paw handed me a little heart pin done in a deep vermilion. Whoever had done it had done it well, because there was even cloisonné white lace on the heart. "Your auntie Pam gave this to me a long time ago."

"It's appropriate." I grinned.

"Shall I make it official?" Dad took the heart from me.

He was a pretty good father, cherry tree and all. Nothing flashy but always steady. He would never hurt anyone, and I was coming to realize that was very important. "Please."

He fumbled with the pin and managed to put the spike through material of my collar. I took the holder from him and put it over the pin's end.

For a little time and space, I thought I would enjoy our charade too. "Thank you," I said, hugging him.

When I sat down again, Tai-Paw picked up her mug of chocolate. "I need to ask you a favor," she said to Dad.

"You name it, you got it," he said in his breezy way.

"It's a big one," Tai-Paw warned.

Dad got a bag of miniature marshmallows and plopped several into her mug. "Name it."

"One other thing," Tai-Paw warned, "you can't tell Casey. She . . . wouldn't understand."

Mom was a professional worrywart who was, is, and forever would be too serious to play at anything. Dad, on the other hand, was like a small, mischievous boy. Just the whiff of a conspiracy was enough to bring a twinkle to his eye. "You got it."

As a reward, Tai-Paw took some of the marshmallows from the bag I had placed on the table and dropped them into Dad's mug. If Dad had adopted her as a surrogate grandmother, she treated him as a favorite grandchild. In fact, Mom was right when she accused Tai-Paw of usually taking Dad's side in any discussion.

"What we need now," she explained, "is to put some kind of bug on the pin so we can track it." I guess she had been watching too many television detectives. "You know all about that electronic stuff. Can you make something?"

Dad laughed. "The only bugs I handle are in software programs." He deposited some marshmallows in my cup as well. "But I used to be pretty handy in chemistry back in high school. I can rig up something low-tech that will be just as useful." He turned to me. "Have you got an old sweater you don't care about?"

"I've got one I was going to donate to Goodwill," I volunteered.

"Wear that tomorrow," he instructed me.

"Sure. Why?"

"Just do it for me," he said. Getting up, he kissed first me on the cheek and then Tai-Paw. After getting some paper coffee filters, he disappeared into the first-floor bathroom.

Everything would be ready for school except me. "Tai-Paw, have your friends ever let you down?"

She tilted back her head and pursed her lips. "Many times. But the other choice is so much worse. So you forgive them—just like you hope they forgive you."

I propped my elbows on the table. "What if you found out what they really thought of you—and it wasn't very nice?"

Mom would have said something about their not

being friends after all; but Tai-Paw had a different way of looking at things. "You hope you do something to change their minds."

I was such a wreck inside that I knew I wasn't up to waiting that long. "But in the meantime you're pretending that you don't care what they think. Maybe you even act like they're your friends. Isn't that living out a lie?" When Tai-Paw started to smile, I snapped suspiciously, "Why are you grinning?"

Tai-Paw put her hand apologetically upon my shoulder. "You're just like your grandmother and mother were at your age. Either a thing was true or it was a lie. There was no in-between. It always hurt them when they found out that most things were both."

I drew my eyebrows together, puzzled. Sometimes talking to Tai-Paw could make you feel like you were on slippery sand. "How can something be true and false at the same time?"

Tai-Paw shifted on her chair. "I had this friend. She was a waitress. When she finished at one restaurant in Chinatown, she would go to another to work. She worked every day at two places. But she was very smart and bought the right property, so she became a real big shot. When I sold my owl charm, my friend told me I should get smart. I should sell it and invest my money like her. Then I could be a big shot too and own a house so big, you could all live with me. She told me I should think of myself."

I remembered the heirloom that Mr. Jeh had copied. Mom had shown the real one to me on a visit to a San Francisco museum where it was kept now. It had impressed me even back then, when I was five. "Why didn't you?"

One corner of her mouth twisted up in an odd sort of smile as she absently massaged the empty space beneath her throat. "Your grandfather needed some help. And so did some others in the family." She pretended to deal out invisible dollar bills. "So my money goes here and there." She pointed at the ceiling. "Instead of to a house. So my friend says I'm a fool."

She looked so sad that it was my turn to comfort her, and it was a strange experience to give to Tai-Paw rather than to take. It made me feel . . . well, mature; and mature in a way that the school clotheshorses, with all their savvy about fashions, were not.

"She's the fool," I insisted, hugging her; and her clothes, soaked in tiger balm and incense, gave off her scent. "Your friend just sounds selfish."

Tai-Paw hugged me back. "That's because you're thinking like a Chinese. All her American friends would've said I was a stupid old woman." But Tai-Paw

161

did not sound like she regretted spending her money on her family.

I held on to her as if I were drowning, and I promised I would not let her feel neglected anymore. "I'm glad you don't have your own house. I'm glad you're with us."

"Really?" Tai-Paw sounded surprised.

"Of course," I said indignantly.

Tai-Paw caressed my hair. "I wasn't sure."

When I heard her, I felt an immense sadness well up inside me. She must have felt so lonely all this time. And suddenly it put all my problems in perspective. I was the selfish one.

While I tried to find a way to reassure her, Mom finally came back. I held out the bowl toward her. "Dad made some popcorn for us."

Mom clicked her tongue in exasperation. "Does he think he can buy forgiveness with a bowl of popcorn?" Then she sniffed. "But it does smell pretty good." Helping herself to a handful, she suppressed a big yawn. "Where is Father Nature anyway?"

"He went back to a big project," Tai-Paw said. I was surprised at how good at fibbing she was. "You should leave him alone."

Mom was unable to stifle the next yawn. "I'm too groggy to have a good argument anyway, so I think I'm going to hit it. You'd better too, young lady. School tomorrow."

I glanced at the clock and groaned. "Don't remind me."

I saw Mom stiffen when I didn't jump up right away and dash to my bed, so I readied myself for yet another lecture. But something odd happened. Instead of scolding me, she actually forced herself to relax.

She'd also let me see a little of that secret younger Chinatown self. "Don't stay up too late," she said, and started to head for the stairs.

I jumped up from my chair. "Mom?" When she had turned around, I hugged her. "Thanks."

Surprised, she hugged me back. "I couldn't have you and Tai-Paw riding buses all hours of the night."

However, I had been trying to thank her for more than that: for lugging the newspapers as a kid and for all her other struggles. We led such a prosperous life here compared to her life in that tiny studio in Chinatown. Comfort hadn't been handed to her on a silver platter; she had made it happen.

"No," I said fiercely, "I mean, thanks for everything."

"What?" Mom chuckled, puzzled. "You're so sleepy you're punch-drunk." Even so, she clung to me.

I didn't fool myself. There would still be stormy

moments ahead. We were too different for that not to happen; but I thought I understood her a little better, and I thought she understood me, too. It was enough for now.

Thirteen

Mom was still asleep the next morning when Tai-Paw woke me bright and early. "Your father has something to show you," she whispered.

He was down in the kitchen in a white shirt and tie, eating some instant oatmeal. Though it was only ten miles to his job, the roads and freeways dated back to the time when Almaden was mostly orchards. As a result, there was so much traffic that he had to leave early to reach work on time.

Even though it was a dreadful hour to be up, he was humming to himself. "Morning, hon." He used his spoon to point at a bottle and some cotton swabs. "There's a blast from my past. Just be careful with it."

I picked up the small bottle and looked at the purplish-brown solution. There seemed to be a small little packet inside. "What is it?"

"Something I used to cook up in chem lab when I

was in high school." He grinned as the oatmeal dripped from his spoon back into the bowl. "Inside that packet is a paste that I filtered through a piece of coffee filter paper. When it's wet, you can smear it on anything. But when it dries, it becomes unstable and goes off with a bang when you touch it."

I set the bottle back down on the table. "Is it dangerous?"

He tried to take a spoonful of oatmeal and seemed surprised when he found that it had fallen back into the bowl. "Not this tiny bit. Just use one of the swabs to paint the surface of the pin."

I stared at the bottle dubiously. "What'll happen then?"

He dipped his spoon back into his oatmeal. "When the thief grabs it, it'll go off with a bang and sting his or her hand, as well as leave a mark that won't come off. Not even with industrial-strength solvents."

"Perfect," Tai-Paw declared.

"I thought so," Dad said smugly.

Something, though, smelled fishy. "Wait a moment. You took in a bunch of coffee filters," I said. "What happened to those?"

Dad squirmed like a small, guilty boy. "I had to run several batches to make sure, hon."

"And what happened to them?" I demanded. "Did you pour them down the sink?"

Dad glanced at me uncomfortably. "You really are getting to be more like your mother. No, I thought I'd bring them in to work and liven things up."

I sighed. "Just don't blow yourself up, okay?"

"What would be the fun of that?" Dad wondered cheerfully.

He was gone by the time I came back down. I ate a cup of instant oatmeal with Tai-Paw and then showed her what I had thought up. "I'll wear the sweater like this," I explained, draping it over my back and tying the arms around my neck. I'd already attached the heart to the sweater. "Then I'll show the heart to everyone and leave it somewhere after I carefully paint it with Dad's stuff."

Tai-Paw grunted her approval. "Good luck."

Getting up to make my lunch, I kissed her on the cheek. "I don't know who's enjoying this more, you or Dad."

"We know how to have a good time," she assured me.

Because I had to wear my backpack, I wore the sweater for the ride to school. Outside, Karen's sharp eyes immediately saw the pin on my sweater. "That's new," she said.

I smoothed down the lapel of my jacket. "Someone special gave it to me."

Karen's jaw dropped open. "No." She flopped onto

her bicycle seat, thunderstruck, and then bounced forward like some jack-in-the-box. "Who is it?"

"Yeah, who is it?" Jeff asked as he came up on his skateboard.

I hesitated. The one drawback to Tai-Paw's plan was that I had to draw attention to myself when I still wanted to hide in my room. And yet if I wanted to uncover the truth, I had to be just like the old Stacy.

"Someone very, very special in my life," I said, polishing the sides with my fingers. "I wouldn't trade it for a diamond ring."

"He's a lucky guy," Jeff said.

"How are you and Cindy?" I asked cautiously.

"That's over for good," Jeff said gloomily. "She's taken up with somebody else. From the debate club yet—and a Young Republican."

"And a fifty-dollar haircut," I teased.

For once, though, the class clown couldn't manage a smile. "Yeah. I grew it long for her."

Karen didn't say anything the rest of the way to school, and usually she was babbling away, which really was her problem. She was basically a sweet person, but she was so talkative that everyone avoided her. The funny thing was that Jeff didn't speak either.

What I didn't figure on was how many other people would notice the pin. I never wore jewelry and never observed what other people wore. Sylvia, though, noticed the pin and made a point of asking about it—as if in her own way she were trying to apologize. Last night I had figured out what to say, so I told her how special it was.

The school gossip, Trish, overheard us and sidled up. "Who's it from?"

"From a friend," I said.

Sylvia nudged Jeff. "You dog. You didn't wait long after Cindy dumped you."

Trish picked up on the idea and teased me. "I didn't know Jeff was your type, Stacy."

"It's not Jeff," I said.

"Su-u-ure," Trish said.

If Trish knew something, then the whole school would. I had wanted her to spread the word about the pin, but I hadn't allowed for Jeff. This little trap was catching me as well. It seemed to be his excuse to reveal he wanted to be more than friends.

When I started to say something, Jeff grabbed my arm. "Never mind."

"Actually I came over to warn you," Trish said to Jeff. "*She* is actually back on campus."

Jeff looked blank. "She?"

So she had kept her word. I had to hand it to her for courage. "You mean Hong Ch'un?" I asked Trish.

Trish studied the pin so she could describe it later

when she spread the gossip. "The same. Can you imagine? What nerve. The whole school is buzzing about it."

Idly Jeff spun a wheel on his skateboard. "Thanks for the warning. I'll watch out for her."

"It's Stacy who ought to watch out." Trish flicked her eyes toward the pin meaningfully as she left.

I looked up at him. "Why didn't you let me tell the truth?"

Jeff grinned. "It'll really put a burn on Cindy."

Well, if he was using me to get back at Cindy, I could use him to set up my thief.

"Lunch?" He held up a fingertip.

I pressed my fingertip against his. "Lunch."

I turned to say something to Karen, but she was already gone.

Once I had my backpack in my locker, I took off my sweater and wore it behind me. Whether it was Trish in action or just the oddity of seeing me sport some jewelry, I got comments in homeroom—even from Ms. Arnold, who pointed it out to the whole class. "I've heard of wearing your heart on your sleeve, but not on your shoulder."

Blushing, I could feel heads swiveling. And for a moment, I almost took the pin off and tried to end it. Somehow I managed to say, "Yes, it's from someone special."

The whistles and catcalls made me wonder about the trap all over again; but I played it out. However, something in me made me begin to dread lunch.

The rest of the morning, I had to endure teasing. Hong Ch'un was at her locker at lunchtime. "That pin is very pretty," she said, and asked a silent question with her eyebrows.

I nodded a silent answer. "It's a gift," I said. "How were things today?"

"Rough, but nothing I couldn't handle," she said. She came from stock just as tough as Tai-Paw. I could see why they had gotten along.

As I got my lunch, I could feel Trish's eyes watching me as I walked off. In a stall in the girls' rest room, I carefully painted the pin and then draped the sweater behind me again.

As I dropped the bottle in the rest room trash can, I wondered how long the stuff would take to dry. I just hoped it wouldn't be while I was wearing it. Once outside, I headed for Jeff's locker, but he found me. "Still want to go through with it?"

"What?" I asked. I was so caught up in the plan I misunderstood his question.

He inclined his head slightly. "Lunch."

"Sure," I said, relieved.

"Where do you want to eat?" he asked obligingly.

"Somewhere not crowded, but where we can be seen," I said.

"Let's try the field, then," Jeff suggested.

Aware of the stares, we made our way through the crowd over to the field and the bleachers. As we sat down, I realized too late that I should have picked up some pizza when we were near the cafeteria. "I hope you've got something decent for lunch. All I could find was rabbit food."

Opening his lunch bag, Jeff produced a package of Twinkies with a flourish. "Behold."

I peered into his bag. There were some miniature chocolate-coated doughnuts and other junk food. "Can we swap mothers?"

Jeff put a finger to his lips. "You wouldn't want what she packed. I stopped by a 7-Eleven on the way here."

I studied Jeff. "You're really a very thoughtful person." I hoped the thief wasn't Jeff as I took off my sweater and laid it on a bench.

"Sylvia told me what that guy called you yesterday. She felt real bad. We don't all think like that jerk," Jeff said.

Since he had raised the subject, I thought it was fair to ask, "But what would you think if you first saw me?"

"What would you think of me?" He flipped his

long hair with the back of his hand. "Surfer bum?"

"I suppose we all make assumptions from appearances," I had to admit.

And if someone looks different, you might tease them about it—like I might tease someone about their freckles. I had made my own assumptions about Hong Ch'un, after all.

"The point is not to think those assumptions are carved in stone," he said.

I was ready to junk those assumptions about Hong Ch'un once I had gotten to know her. However, some jerks you can't get to change their minds because you can't change what doesn't exist.

Now I supposed I was doing my own stereotyping about bigots. It's a funny thing about bigots. Most of them aren't pure monsters. For one thing, bigots can be nice to dogs. Bigots are probably nice to their families and friends, too. Even so, there are holes in their souls where there ought to be hearts.

However, it was reassuring to hear that Jeff still accepted me. There would always be some jerks in the world. I could only hope that the Jeffs outnumbered them.

Leaning forward, I rapped my knuckles against his forehead. "Naw, that's not stone. Sounds like solid wood to me."

"Knotty pine, to be precise." He took another paper

napkin from the bag and draped it over his arm as if he were a waiter. "The special for the day is beer nuts."

"You really know how to spoil a girl," I said.

He frowned distastefully at the lunch in my open bag. "A healthy one at any rate."

Lunch, actually, was not as much fun as other times we'd had. I think I was a little too self-conscious. With forced cheer, I asked Jeff what he had for dessert after Twinkies.

"You wash it down with this." And he pulled an orange water pistol out of his bag. "I already had this in my locker." Jeff's aim was almost as perfect as his timing. The first squirt caught me right in my open mouth. As I sat there, spluttering, he doused me in the face.

"This is for having secrets from a friend," he whispered.

"Stop," I said, spitting out a mouthful of water. I lunged for the pistol, but he shot off the bench.

"Who is he?" He sprayed my hair so that I must have looked like a drowned rat. "Tell me."

Blinking the water from my eyes, I rose. "You jerk."

I jumped off the bleachers and started to chase him. Of course, it would have helped if I could have seen better, but he kept squirting me unerringly in the face. "Okay, okay," he finally said, "I've had my revenge."

I wiped my eyes on my damp sleeve. I didn't think

it was mercy that made him stop. "Out of water?"

He held the pistol aimed at his head and pulled the trigger. A drop of water trickled out. "How'd you guess?"

I stormed toward the bleachers. "Have you got any more napkins in your bag?"

"I put in a dozen." He paralleled my course, keeping well out of kicking range.

When we got back to the bleachers I got the napkins from his bag and wiped my face. "How can I go to class like this?"

Jeff picked up my sweater and held it out to me. "Put this on."

I'd been so mad at his trick that I'd almost forgotten the whole purpose of my being out there. The pin was gone. Carefully I checked the sweater, but it wasn't anywhere. I probably hadn't heard the bang because I'd been too busy shouting at Jeff. "My dad gave me that pin," I said.

"I'm sorry, Stace. I don't see it anywhere." He straightened as a new thought occurred to him. "Do you think the thief has struck again?"

I glanced down. If he had taken the pin, there would have been stains on his fingers, but his fingertips were clean. "I'm going to find out. If you had something on your fingers, what's the first thing you'd do?"

"Wash it off," he said.

"If you do me a big favor," I said, "I'll forgive you for what you just did."

"Sure."

"Check the boys' rest rooms and look for anyone trying to wash stains from their fingers. He'll be the thief."

"So that's it." Jeff held up his hands as a new thought occurred to him. "You checked my fingers first, didn't you?" The accusation and hurt were plain in his voice.

I had learned a few tricks from Mom in my time. "What makes you angry? That I suspected you?"

He seemed surprised by the question. "We *were* friends."

I noticed the past tense. "But we *are* friends. Suspicion is something that friends can talk around and make up over."

"Next time I try to argue with a shrink's daughter, shoot me." He threw his arms up in surrender. "So what are you going to do in the meantime?"

"Check the girls' rest rooms." I went into high gear, speeding across the asphalt.

Fourteen

I ducked into the girls' rest room in the gym, but there was no one there.

Dodging in and out among students and ignoring their comments on my wet clothes, I got to the rest room on the eastern side of campus. One of the school clotheshorses, Trish, was there. She had her makeup, brushes, and other things laid out before her like a surgeon preparing for a heart transplant.

When she saw me staring at her hands, she turned. "What's up?"

Her hands were clean.

With a growing sense of urgency, I raced through the laughing students by the cafeteria. The door to the auditorium was locked, but I dashed around the side to try the rear door. That one was open, and though the auditorium was dark, I knew my way well enough to stumble along until I reached the girls' rest room there.

My heart stopped when I heard the sound of water running. When I jerked the door open, I hated to look inside.

It was Sylvia. She gave a jump when she saw it was me. "Oh, Stacy," she said, "you startled me."

I felt as awkward as she did. "Did you see anyone come in here?"

With her arms held behind her, she tried to block my view of the sink. "No, there's just me."

"What're you doing? Cleaning up?" I craned my neck.

"No, just trying to get some privacy." Facing me, she began to shuffle sideways from the sink but halted abruptly. "Ow."

A can dropped on the floor and began to roll. Lifting my foot, I stopped it; but when I reached down, Sylvia put her hand on my wrist. "Careful. It's awfully hot. That's why I dropped it."

Lifting my shoe, I stared at the bright, gaudy label with the little blue creatures running around. It was a can of Smurf-shaped spaghetti.

Sheepishly Sylvia went over to the hot water tap and turned it off. "Every now and then I get a hankering for this. I can't really say why. So I sneak in here and run hot water over it to heat it."

Sylvia's hands were sparkling clean. "I know how cravings are," I agreed.

Sylvia licked her lips desperately. "If you won't tell anyone, I'll make it worth your while, Stacy."

I held up my hands. "I'll take the secret to my grave," I said, zipping my lips for emphasis.

Sylvia's shoulders sagged with relief. "How about brownies? More of them than you can eat?"

Somehow brownies didn't seem like such an awful bribe. "We'll have a party." I grinned and left, leaving Sylvia to her guilty pleasure.

As I stood uncertainly outside the auditorium, I thought again about what Dad had told me when he had presented the stuff to me: Normal soap wouldn't remove it. In fact, he had talked about industrial-strength solvents. So perhaps the thief was already looking for some stronger cleaner like that.

I was off and running again, this time to the janitor's building, which was about a hundred yards away, past the Dumpsters.

The janitors had their lockers in a square white building where the furnace was. To keep out vandals, the windows were small and set up high, out of climbing range. At the moment, though, all the janitors were out policing the campus.

From handling the aftermath of various campus functions, I knew where the mops and cleaning stuff were. In front of me, I heard water pouring into a metal sink. Almost tripping on the mops in the buckets, I jerked the door open. There, scrubbing furiously at her hands over a sink, was Karen.

In a way I was sorry to see that our trap had worked. She was the one friend I could count on. So I felt like I had lost even when I had won. Just like the Thief of Hearts. "Why, Karen?"

She turned away from the sink with her hands behind her back. "Why what?"

There was an open can of cleanser next to the sink. The pungent smell filled the air. "You know what." I took a step into the room. "You're the thief."

She took a step back and tried to act innocent. "What makes you say that?"

"Let me see your hands, Karen." I walked toward her.

"You can't boss me around." Karen backed up against the wall.

"I'm not trying to." I paused by the sink and turned off the tap. "I'm just trying to find who took some valuable property."

"Go talk to your skinny Chinese friend," Karen insisted.

I held out my palms. "It's no use trying to hide anymore."

Karen lifted her chin defiantly. "Who needs to hide? You and your big-shot friends never notice me anyway."

"That's not true," I said calmly.

Karen got so angry that she drew her hands from behind her back and balled them into fists. "Don't patronize me. I've got eyes. I can see what happens. It wasn't so bad when they ignored me because they never paid me any attention, but when you started to ignore me, that was too much. You went to school with that Chinese girl, but we always go to school together."

"It was my father's idea," I pointed out. "I didn't have any choice."

"You've known me longer," Karen said; the hurt was plain in her voice. "But you just rode away with her."

And suddenly I thought I saw what started it. "So you decided to frame her."

"No." Karen gave her head a savage shake. "She's the thief." She shrank back against the wall with her hands behind her back again.

I smiled patiently. "I know it was you, Karen."

Karen squirmed against the wall. "Those people who lost things had it coming. They all thought they were so hot, but they're just like all the rest of us. You take one thing and it hurts them just like they hurt other people."

"Sylvia can say mean things," I admitted. "And Jeff plays pranks. But Mr. Barrows?"

"He's really not very fair," Karen said. "People work

real hard and try to make friends with people who ignore them, and then he tells parents that their children aren't very sociable."

"That isn't very fair," I agreed sympathetically.

Karen was close to tears. "And then Jeff gave you that pin. So you were going to shut me out."

"And so you finally stole from me," I said quietly.

Karen shook her head silently.

"Let me see your hands, Karen." My palms turned upward, I wriggled my fingers at her. "Come on. Let me see."

Karen huddled with her arms hidden behind her. "No."

"Karen, I won't ever stop being your friend no matter what you've done." Feeling the irony of it, I crossed my own heart swiftly with my left hand. "I swear, Karen."

Mutely, Karen slowly brought her hands around to the front. I turned the clenched fists over and slowly pried the fingers apart. The tips were stained a bright purple.

"How did you plant the other things in her backpack?" I asked.

Karen lowered her hands. "You never cover up your lock when you open it. Anyone could have learned your combination."

"Give back my heart, Karen," I said gently.

Karen freed her right hand and reached into the pocket of her jeans. "You won't tell?"

I took the little heart back. All of Dad's stuff had worn off, so it was safe to handle now. "I have to, Karen. You can't let Hong Ch'un be persecuted."

"I don't know what got into me," she blurted out. "I just got so mad. And then . . . and then . . ."

". . . it snowballed," I finished for her.

She shrugged her shoulders silently. "So please don't tell. Please. Please. You know my parents."

I got a lump in my throat remembering all the good times we'd had when we were small. "I'll help. My mom will help," I promised.

And suddenly Karen was crying and hugging me. "It'll be okay," I said as I patted her on the back.

"Hey!" We turned to see Harold, the head janitor, in gray coveralls and an A's cap. "You kids get out of here!"

"Sorry, Harold." I ushered Karen out of there like a mother hen with her chick.

Fifteen

There were other missing items in Karen's locker, and after I had left her with Mr. Barrows, I made a point of returning each item and making sure that its owner knew who the thief really was and that it wasn't Hong Ch'un.

When school was finished, I found Hong Ch'un chatting in a friendly way with Sylvia and a couple of other girls. Although the pendulum had swung so far to the wrong side, maybe it would swing the right way now and students would make a point of talking to her. For her part, Hong Ch'un seemed to be making a special effort to get along.

"Are you going to try out for the track team?" asked a girl called Luisa.

"Perhaps," Hong Ch'un said cautiously.

"You don't want to tire out those legs before the dance," Sylvia warned her.

"I don't know American dances," Hong Ch'un said shyly.

"I'll show you," Luisa said.

"Your moves are all so geeky," Miranda teased her, and promised Hong Ch'un, "I better show you, honey."

The funny thing was, it was almost as if Hong Ch'un and I had traded places, and I was now the outsider. I felt a hundred years old as I went to my locker.

When she saw me, Hong Ch'un excused herself. "Stacy."

"Yeah?" I asked as I got my backpack from the locker.

"Thank you," she said, and bowed.

It was so unexpected that at first I didn't know what to do. "Forget it."

"I can't. It was like a bad dream," she said, "but you made it come out all right."

I began to stuff books into my backpack. "Part of the trouble was your own doing," I said.

"I know," she admitted. "I didn't want to leave China. I was so scared. Things are so different here. I didn't want to change."

I shouldered my backpack. When Hong Ch'un let down her guard, she was really pretty nice. Maybe we'd be friends one day. "You seem like a fast learner now."

"Thank you," she said, "but what can I do to repay you?"

At first I was going to tell her to forget it, but I stopped. "Forgive Karen," I said. "And try to be her friend."

There was a slight time lag while she figured out what I had said. Even after she understood, she still hesitated and then smiled. "Your help is expensive, but I will—and I'll try to be yours, too."

I told myself I shouldn't make assumptions about her any more than people made them about Karen. "I'd like that," I said, and locked my locker.

I called Mom and lucked out by getting her when she was free. "I'm so sorry," she said when I told her who the thief was.

I thought of Karen's strange home with the dueling televisions. "Her parents are going to kill her." I didn't mean literally, of course; but I could just imagine the sort of things they'd call her now.

Mom knew about them too. "I think Karen's real problem is low self-esteem. She doesn't need a psychologist; she just needs to improve her situation at home, and that means the whole family. I can recommend a good family counselor. Debbie would even do it pro bono if I asked. The only problem is that I can't see how we could get Karen's parents to go."

I cradled the phone against my ear, beginning to hope. "What if you got Mr. Barrows to talk to them? I bet the Perskys would go if it meant Karen wouldn't get kicked out of school."

"That just might work," Mom agreed. "You're getting pretty devious, do you know that?"

"Hey," I chuckled, "I'm the daughter of a shrink." And I hung up. It was a small hope for my friend, but things wouldn't change until the Perskys all took that first step.

I couldn't wait to get home and tell Tai-Paw, but when I got there, I found a strange car in our driveway. It was one of those old gas-guzzling Cadillacs that look as big as whales. The white Caddy even had fins on the fenders.

I circled it, trying to figure out who owned it, but I couldn't match it up with any of my parents' friends. On the right lower corner of the rear window was a sticker of an orange-and-purple lion's head. Still puzzled, I went to the front door. Even through the thick wood paneling I could hear a loud clattering sound.

More bewildered than ever, I opened the front door. Tai-Paw was talking happily in Chinese over the clack-clack-clack. I was surprised, though, when a woman answered her back.

"Tai-Paw?" I asked.

"In here," Tai-Paw called.

I followed the noise into the living room. Mr. Jeh was there with a Chinese man and woman in their seventies. "Hello," Mr. Jeh said.

They had set up Mom's pink card table so that Tai-Paw could break out her Mah-Jong set. She and Mom had tried to get me to play, so I knew the rules were a little bit like those of gin rummy; but I hadn't cared for it very much.

They were busy mixing up all the little tiles before assembling them in a square with two-tile-high walls—the equivalent to shuffling and dealing the cards. It was so long since Tai-Paw had last broken out her set that the sound was unfamiliar.

Tai-Paw was happily sweeping her hands in circular motions so that the tiles were thoroughly jumbled together—and making the clattering noise I had heard. "We have visitors."

Mr. Jeh waved his hand to indicate first Tai-Paw and then me. "You not come to Chinatown. Chinatown come to you." He swung his hand to the man. "This my nephew Sherman and that his wife, Shirley. I tell them, 'Stop counting all your money and drive me down here.'"

Sherman was a fat man with thinning hair. In his mouth he had a huge unlit cigar, which he then yanked back out to talk. "Anything to see Mrs. Low—though you'd think she'd be gracious enough to let me win a game."

"Friendship is friendship," Tai-Paw observed, "and Mah-Jong is Mah-Jong."

I was pleased that Mr. Jeh had included me as part of his goal; but I wasn't sure about the other two. "How do you do," I said with polite formality.

Sherman sized me up in a quick glance. "So you're Casey's kid. You look just like her." He appealed to Shirley. "Doesn't she, honey?"

Shirley studied me with open but friendly curiosity. "Don't tell your mom, but I think you're prettier."

After yesterday, I had been expecting anything but flattery. "You know my mom?"

"We never had a better clerk in our store." Sherman sliced the air with his cigar. "She could sell anything." He turned again to his wife to reminisce. "Remember the gross of quartz cicadas your brother stuck us with?"

"It was two gross," Shirley corrected him amiably, "and it was your brother, Farragut, who dumped them on us."

"Whatever." Sherman waved his cigar vaguely. "Couldn't give the darn things away until she looked up what the Chinese used to use them for. When folks asked me what they were for, I'd say they were for good luck; but she told us that the Chinese carved them out of jade and put them on the tongues of the dead."

I was still busy digesting yet another bit of history about Mom. "Really?"

"In the old, old days, the Chinese used to believe jade could keep things pure so they wouldn't decay." Shirley picked up a handful of tiles and began to stack them. "And cicadas were symbols of resurrection because real cicadas come out of the ground periodically."

As if it were a signal, the others also started to build a wall of tiles in front of themselves.

"Whatever," Sherman said. "Well, your mom would home in on a customer and spin out such a yarn that I'd even want to buy one. When she'd see a prospect, she'd sink her teeth in and there was no shaking her off. She was like a bulldog." He sighed with admiration. "Sales were never the same once she went off to college."

I suppose Mom had brought the same intensity to selling cicadas as she had to shrinking brains. "No kidding."

"She didn't leave us until she attended graduate school," Shirley corrected him.

"Whatever," Sherman said amiably, and restored the cigar between his lips.

Tai-Paw waved me over. "So what happened to-day?"

"It worked," I said. "It was Karen."

Tai-Paw understood my hurt. "Oh, I'm sorry."

I shrugged out of my backpack and dumped it on the floor. It landed with a leaden thud—just like the way my soul felt. "I feel like it's my fault. If I'd paid her more attention, she wouldn't have tried to steal it. And then I'm the one who set the trap that caught her."

Tai-Paw rose slowly from the chair. "Excuse me," she said to her guests. "Go ahead and play without me."

"Sure thing," Sherman said. "Maybe I'll win for a change."

"It's all right," I said to her. "You've got guests."

She took my arm in her unbreakable grip. "No, I want to talk."

We went into the hallway past Dad's study to her room. She had left the television on, so all the way I could hear a Chinese mystery show echoing in the corridor.

"They caught me by surprise," she explained. A cup half full of tea sat on a TV tray beside her recliner.

"It's really all right," I tried to tell her.

I couldn't lie to her any more than I could lie to myself.

"Don't try to take on the whole world. You're too young."

It had been a long time since I had been in the room, which had her concentrated scent. In a corner was a bureau upon which photos of her many children, grandchildren, and great-grandchildren mingled with the statues of various Chinese gods. It almost looked like a party.

One statue was a serene-looking woman who had a flower in her hands. Another was of a fat, bald man who looked quite happy as children climbed over him. There was also a group of eight small statues that each held something. One had a sword, another a fan, and so on. Another was of a bald man with a huge dome for a head. I made yet another note to myself to ask about some of the statues.

Right in front of the dome-headed statue stood a photo of Mom and Dad and me when I was ten. It was a photo I particularly hated because I had made the mistake of showing my teeth when I smiled, and the light had bounced off my braces.

"What if there isn't a world anymore?" I just stood there, knowing that my safe little universe had come apart and feeling my joints and limbs ache in sympathetic pain—and knowing that there was no way to put things back together, either in that universe or in me.

Mom would have analyzed me. Dad would have tried to make it better by taking me out and buying me something. Tai-Paw, though, just studied me thoughtfully. "I'm sorry you had to grow up so fast. I watched my children grow up fast. My grandchildren grew up even faster. And you great-grandchildren grow up the fastest of all." She pantomimed a plant growing taller by the second. "And I want to tell you not to grow so fast, because I know there are all sorts of nasty hurts out there. I want to protect you a little longer. But you grow up anyway."

She released me and shuffled over toward her television. "When Jeanie died, I wanted to die too." Jeanie was her daughter and my grandmother. "A mother's not supposed to outlive her children."

Drawn to her, I drifted over to her side. "But you lived."

"Casey came." She smiled at the memory. "And then you."

I thought again of Hong Ch'un and the Dumpster crew. "Even if I'm a mixed seed?"

"Don't listen to small-minded people," Tai-Paw said. "They judge people by looks. They don't understand how big the world really is. Someday it will shock them."

"Your friends Sherman and Shirley didn't seem shocked to see me," I recalled.

She jabbed at a button, turning off the television. "They shouldn't. Their daughter married a nice American boy. And they have very smart, very pretty grandchildren. That kind of marriage wasn't so common then, but it happens plenty now."

I remembered Mr. Jeh's offer. "Would you walk with me through Chinatown, or would you be ashamed?"

"What kind of talk is that?" She laced her fingers with mine. "I'd show you off. You're so pretty and smart. And if they said anything, we wouldn't need Mr. Jeh. I'd take care of them myself."

And I realized she loved me no matter what I was or what I did; she had always loved me completely and unconditionally. So I hugged her. Through all her layers of clothes, she was as solid as rock. Come storm or flood, I'd be okay as long as I could hold on to her. Cities might vanish and empires might crumble, but I could count on her heart to always see the way. It was something that went beyond labels like Chinese and American.

Maybe I'd never have a home like Chinatown. Maybe I'd be as rootless as Dad; but that didn't matter. We make our own homes. The people we meet are the bricks, and love is the cement. With Mom and Dad and Tai-Paw I had a pretty good start. And there were old friends like Jeff and new friends like Mr. Jeh and Gilbert.

From outside I heard Shirley shout, *"Pung!"*

Sherman boomed out something in loud, exasperated Chinese, and both he and Mr. Jeh began complaining loudly about the tiles they had drawn.

"Come on. Maybe your guests ought to take a time out and have some hot chocolate." I started to pull her out of the room.

"Ice cream sundaes would be nicer," she said as she shuffled after me.

Afterword

It has been some eighteen years since *Child of the Owl* was published, but it has been some thirty years since the time period in which it was set, for I deliberately set Chinatown in the pre-1965 period, before the immigration laws were changed. The Chinatown I knew as a boy was very much like a small town, with all of a small town's strengths and flaws, and that is the Chinatown of that novel. During this period, Chinatown was synonymous with being a Chinese American.

And yet at the time I wrote the novel *Child of the Owl*, I could see how the influx of Asian immigrants was changing Chinatown. In addition, the enforcement of Fair Housing laws and patterns of investment allowed Chinatown to expand beyond its traditional borders, and the increased opportunities have had a centrifugal effect. Most of my classmates from St. Mary's Chinese School now live in the suburbs, or in other areas of San Francisco.

I also wished to write about another change that I have seen since the sixties. There was a time in California when it was against the law for Asian Americans to marry whites. Even after that law was rescinded, there were social pressures on both sides that worked against mixed marriages. When I was a child, many people in Chinatown assumed that one would marry another Chinese American. However, since that time many of my schoolmates and friends have married people of other races—myself included. Living in San Francisco and visiting schools, I can see that there is a new generation growing up with its own unique questions, when we have only started to answer the old ones.